THE GOLDEN CAGE

Urdu Short Stories
by Asian Women in Britain

of allied interest

From Across The Shores
Punjabi Short Stories
by Asians in Britain

Translated into English &
Critical Introduction by
RANA NAYAR

The Golden Cage

Urdu Short Stories by Asian Women in Britain

Foreword by

Dr. Ranjana Sidhanta Ash

Translated and Compiled by

SAFIA SIDDIQI

Soma Books Ltd. • London
Paramount Books (P) Ltd. • Karachi
Sterling Publishers (P) Ltd. • New Delhi

Published in U.K. by
SOMA BOOKS LTD.
38 Kennington Lane, London SE 11 4LS
Tel: 44(0) 20 77352101 Fax: 44(0) 20 77353076
E-mail: books@somabooks.co.uk
ISBN: 0861449525

Published in Pakistan by
PARAMOUNT BOOKS (PVT) LTD.
152/0, Block 2, PECH Society, Karachi 75400
Tel: 92 21 4310030 Fax: 00 92 21 4553772
E-mail: paramount@cyber.net.pk
ISBN: 969 494123 7

Published in India and for rest of the World by
STERLING PUBLISHERS PRIVATE LIMITED
A-59, Okhla Industrial Area, Phase-II, New Delhi-110020
Tel : 6916209, 6916165, 6912677, 6910050 Fax: 6331241
E-mail: ghai@nde.vsnl.net.in
www.sterlingpublishers.com
ISBN 81 207 2415 1

The Golden Cage: Urdu Short Stories
by Asian Women in Britain

Printed in India
Line drawings by Sunil Handa

Foreword

It gives me such pleasure to write a foreword for Safia Siddiqi's translations of stories written in Urdu by women, mainly of Pakistani origin, now settled in Britain. The special value of Safia's anthology entitled *The Golden Cage* lies in the selection of writing by women of the South Asian diaspora in Britain, who had to leave their families to make new homes in British cities like London, Manchester and Bradford. Outside their language domain these women have continued to write in Urdu, their preferred creative medium, though most of them would have been educated in both English and Urdu before migration.

Loyalty to home languages must be one of the most distinctive features of South Asian migration to Britain. Urdu and five other major languages of the Indian subcontinent — Bengali, Gujarati, Hindi, Punjabi and Tamil — are not only used orally at home but also cultivated as the media of journalism and literature. Literary events where poetry and short fiction are read and reviewed, the publication of novels and anthologies, and the effort to teach members of the younger generation their community languages, are pursued vigorously. Safia's work has the added value of presenting some of this creative effort in English translation for the benefit of a British readership ignorant of Urdu. It is a pioneering venture that should be emulated by women from other linguistic minorities.

The stories have been written from two separate but interlinked perspectives: that of the displaced and uprooted immigrant, homesick and lonely, trying to adjust to the new ways of living in a cold, and often unfriendly, racist neighbourhood, and that of women becoming increasingly aware of changing values and the burden of traditional constraints imposed on wives by husbands following patriarchal norms and authoritarian ways with greater fervour, when fearful of their erosion in permissive Britain.

It is this combination, of a feminist gaze that recognises the desire to maintain familial norms while, at the same time, being aware of the imbalance between the changing attitudes of husband and wife, that creates tension in these narratives. There are a few stories of outright violence directed at the women. Others show the effect of change on the traditional notions of morality which permits men to violate customary taboos while forcing women to adhere to the most rigid rules of modesty and domestic discipline. Hovering around everything is the steady pressure of British economic realities and the weakening of family ties leaving the elderly at the mercy of second generation British-Asian sons and daughters-in-law. While the feminist concerns of most of the writers in the anthology is not overt or accentuated, it runs like an undercurrent through the entire collection, treated with detachment and irony in some stories or with emotional intensity in others.

All the writers selected, except one, are Muslim women. What makes this fact particularly significant for a readership, conditioned by ignorance and a prejudiced depiction of Islam in Britain, lies in the varied space given to religion by these writers. Revealed more through cultural norms than a devout injunction, these stories show aspects of compassion, beautifully depicted in the ones written by Firoza Jaffer and Naeema Ziauddin.

Ranjana Sidhanta Ash*

**Dr. R. S. Ash is a freelance writer and translator.*

TRANSLATOR'S NOTE

This is a collection of translated stories originally written by Indian and Pakistani women now settled in Britain. The writers had been feeling, for quite some time, that there was a need to have a translation of their stories, which were written in Urdu, their mother tongue. These writers, who have been living here, working here, and bringing up their children in this country, through their experiences, inspiration and observations have a unique value for people who want an insight into the Asian community. They have experienced the pain of uprootedness, the humiliation of racial prejudice and have deeply felt the clash of cultures and its impact on their lives. Their emotions are raw and real in this collection; the stories mostly focus on their own community, its behaviour, its double standards, and the realisation that women have to bear the brunt of it all. They are also a mirror of what is happening in the Asian community and how the first generation of immigrants from the Indian subcontinent perceives living, and experiences life, in the West.

Safia Siddiqi

ACKNOWLEDEGMENTS

My special thanks to Dr. Ranjana Ash for reading and editing the translated stories and writing the foreword.

Heartfelt thanks to Dr. Firoze Mookerji, a dear friend, for her useful advice and whole-hearted support throughout a difficult and laborious period.

I am also extremely grateful to Najma Usman, a close friend, and her colleagues, the ESOL staff of South Thames College, for reading the translation and giving useful remarks and suggestions.

My most profound thanks to Sabiha Qureshi, another close friend, for reading the first draft of the manuscript and giving helpful suggestions and remarks.

Finally, a word of thanks to members of my family. I would have liked to thank my son, Zafar, for providing me with a brand new word processor to work with. Sadly he passed away, before I could complete the work. He continues to live in our hearts.

I would also like to thank my daughter, Naima, and my son, Rizwan, for familiarising me with the computer and its simple but unusual technicalities. Also their help in the translation and setting of the manuscript is very much appreciated.

CONTENTS

SHAHEDA AHMED

THE REVELATION

***Shaheda Ahmed** comes from Lahore, Pakistan, where she grew up and obtained her degree. She came to London after her marriage. She took part in the BBC's Urdu World Service programmes. In 1983, she compiled and published the first collection of Urdu short stories by Asian writers living in the UK. In 1985, she went back to Pakistan where she started a magazine to help those suffering with disabilities and to create awareness about the issues surrounding them. She returned to London in 1989 and participated in a science programme for the BBC's Urdu World Service. Later, she went on to produce and present a children's programme for a local Asian radio. Shaheda writes short stories and plays. Her plays, which she directed herself, have been staged in London and other cities in the UK. She also took part in them. Shaheda has published a novel, a collection of short stories and a stage play. The second collection of her short stories and an autobiography are soon to be published. She lives in Middlesex.*

She put her handbag under the front seat and sat down. Fastening her seat-belt she looked around her with curiosity. When there hadn't been anything interesting to see in Bahrain, what was she going to find in this Gulf Air flight? High temperatures converted the water into steam, and the artificial coolness of air-conditioning had caused her to pass the whole week sneezing away.

"Excuse me," said a tall middle-aged Englishman who was arranging himself on the seat next to her. He looked fiftyish, smart and his greying hair made him look graceful.

"Hello, I am John Smith," fastening his seat-belt, the Englishman introduced himself, looking sideways at his fellow-traveller, smiling.

"I am Frida," she smiled politely in response, and opened her bag kept at her feet and took out a book. It was *A Letter to Christendom*, by Rana Kabani. She opened it where she had placed the bookmark last week, during her journey to Bahrain.

"Are you Egyptian?"

"No, I'm Pakistani," she answered with her eyes set firmly on the book in front of her.

"Do you live here in Bahrain?"

"No, I came here to visit my sister. I live in London."

"Oh, well, I also came for two months in connection with my work."

Frida recognised from his accent that he was from Scotland, but she didn't ask him to confirm it. She continued concentrating on the book she was reading. In the beginning of the book, the scene showed the year of 1492, when the last Muslim Sultan of Spain was down on his knees, presenting the keys of the city of Granada to the Catholic king. It was heart-rending and painful for her to even read about it. It felt like the echo of the wilderness in the pages of the book. But John Smith had had a few drinks and he was in a talkative mood.

"You don't look like a Pakistani lady; not by your looks, and accent, and dress...!"

"Should I regard it as a compliment or an insult?" She was forced to close the book and divert her attention towards this fellow passenger.

"Insult! But why?" he asked innocently and in such a manner that she had no answer. He demanded an answer, "Do tell me why you regarded my question as an insult?"

"Because you don't look like an Englishman to me either, not by your attitude, or the way you speak."

"How can it be?" he exclaimed. "I am an Englishman through and through. My wife is Scottish and that's why I have been living in Scotland for a long time." John Smith pulled out a hip-flask from his pocket, and drank a mouthful of Scotch as he replied.

"But you don't seem to have been affected by it either," Frida said teasingly.

"What do you mean?" He was taken aback.

"I mean if you were a true Englishman, you would have started the conversation with the weather, not with personal remarks about me."

"Ah, well. I have been living with Americans for the last two months, they hold the credit for my manners." He laughed pleasantly, and looked at her with frankness and emotion showing in his eyes.

"How attractive and sweet you are! And my wife, her brows are always furrowed and she always throws cutting remarks at me. The secret of a woman's beauty is her gentleness, and pleasant nature. Just like you — otherwise, without these qualities, a woman is not a woman — she is like someone who is leading an army."

Frida fidgeted, changed her position, but John Smith continued regardless: "Do you know something — I am frightened — of going home. Whenever I do, the thought of my wife terrifies me and I feel as if I am entering the bedroom of a vampire. If I didn't have my girlfriend to escape to, God knows what would have happened."

"Is she so bad, your wife?" Frida asked coolly.

"Even more so — look, I am going home after eight weeks' absence but I don't have the slightest hope of receiving any home comfort or pleasure. Instead, imagining her bitter conversation and harsh attitude frightens me out of my wits. My girlfriend has already booked a hotel room for the weekend, so that I can relax with her."

"If she is so horrible to you why don't you divorce her?" Frida spoke sharply.

"Well, divorce is not allowed in the Catholic faith, and my youngest son still needs his mother. Divorce will upset him, I don't want to mess up his future."

"You mean that keeping a girlfriend is allowed in your religion? The atmosphere you have in your home is a happy one for your son, is it?"

"I don't know," Smith shrugged his shoulders.

"How many children do you have?"

"Three. The eldest one is a qualified doctor now. My daughter is a bank official and the youngest one is doing his 'A' levels," he said proudly.

"The woman who has brought up these clever children could never be a mental case, could she? Perhaps being a housewife has made her bored and quarrelsome." Frida tried to analyse the situation.

"Housewife!" Smith was aghast. "When did I say she was a housewife? No, she is a senior executive in an international monetary organisation. But you cannot imagine, as soon as she sees me, her brows become knitted and the bitterness in her voice increases and the cutting remarks — you just can't imagine it!"

"I can imagine it very well," Frida's icy tone became somewhat mysterious. "You see her as an ageing woman now — her face unattractive, even ugly, don't you?"

"Yes, but how do you know?" he asked looking surprised.

"Don't ask me how I know, just tell me if what I say is true. You wanted to marry her, didn't you?"

"Yes, I did."

"Then she was extremely beautiful — her beauty second to none?"

"Yes."

"Then you were like Maharaj Matari Raj of Rajghari, and you worshipped her like a goddess."

"Who is that?" John Smith asked, amazed.

"He was a Hindu king, and Rani Vijyavanti was his beautiful wife. She gave up her husband's kingdom and went away in the search for eternal truth. When the truth about life was revealed to her, she realised that as man and woman are the two wheels of life, then, unless the woman stands equal to man, the vehicle of life cannot run smoothly." He was even more confused.

"What are you trying to say?"

"Only that she was neither a *maharani* nor a *devi*, a goddess. She would have been a useful working wheel sharing all the burdens of life with you. She wouldn't have tried to be an empty, decorative wheel, would she?"

"Yes, she has always been a very practical person."

"Not only that but she must have been very ambitious?"

"That's also true."

"She must have spent her early married life and youthful years in hardship and in struggle with you. Those days were so bad that even thinking about them makes you shiver."

"Perhaps you are right here too."

"Both of you must have been passionately in love, but on your way to success and prosperity you became distanced from each other. You didn't even realise when and where, and how, a wife who loved her husband with her heart and soul, and would have done anything to make him happy, got lost."

"Well, yes, something like that happened to us."

"Not only that Mr. Smith, much more has happened to you. Now when you are someone and have arrived somewhere, you do not find her attractive. You see only motherhood."

"Too true."

"You see her as a stepmother, not a wife; cruel, unkind and exploiting."

"Yes, yes, it's like that."

"You want your wife, whom you see only as a mother, along with her youthful children, to let you do whatever your heart desires. She should allow you to try to be young and behave like one, and respect your wishes."

"I just don't know," he was like foam settling down.

"Why don't you know Mr. Smith, you know everything. The fact is that your wife is a reminder of the days when you had nothing except an inferiority complex. You hesitated to be proud and boastful about yourself before her. She knew you when your vest and underpants used to have holes in them. You cannot brag about yourself in front of her because she is a souvenir of your past. The middle-aged husband who used to watch *Gone with the Wind* and *Lawrence of Arabia* with his wife, and belonged to the world of *Wall Street Journal* and *The Economist*, now watches *Basic Instinct* with his girlfriend and seems to be more interested in reading the *Cosmopolitan*. The one who used to enjoy the symphonies of Beethoven and Mozart, now passionately converses about Apache Indian — and enters his house to the tune of 'Baby—Baby'. What is your wife going to feel if not being burnt slowly like wet wood? She is not going to welcome you with open arms, is she? You have begun hating your wife because she knows every lie and every truth, and you feel as if there is a hidden meter in her, keeping her informed about your feelings — their high and low voltages."

"But, but, how do you know all about us?" Smith asked, both surprised and worried.

"Because, this woman whom you consider to be very attractive and well-disposed, is also in the same league as your wife, Mr. Smith. The truth is that irrespective of colour and creed, and regardless of the difference of cultures, men behave the same way all over the world. They love their own children and someone else's wife."

And slowly Frida's eyes became clouded with tears.

(The title of the story in Urdu is *Bhedi.*)

SABIHA ALVI

A COMPROMISE

Sabiha Alvi *is from Hyderabad, India. She writes short stories and articles for British magazines and newspapers. She has been taking an Urdu language workshop for schoolchildren and has given lectures on subjects such as why the mother tongue is important for Asian children living in England. She lives in North Wales.*

When Junaid's first letter arrived, the blue aerogramme with the Queen's head printed on it, Humera quickly sat down behind closed doors and read it again and again. Junaid had written about the details of his journey from Bombay to London. He had promised to write more often. Humera was relieved to know that he had reached safely. In those days there were no phones in the houses and also there was no direct line available either. As he had no money to spare he couldn't even send a telegram, or phone. He had somehow managed to go abroad, although it had been very difficult for him to raise the money to buy a ticket. It had just become possible to travel at the eleventh hour.

Junaid couldn't get a job soon after he arrived in London, the reason being that his friends had informed him that the 'job centre' people always sent Indians and Pakistanis for the lowest kind of jobs available, and once you had gone for that you would forever be in it, they had told him. They had advised him to wait for a job which matched his education and experience. Nearly a year went by and he didn't get the one he wanted and had to continue doing temporary jobs. Humera and her children stayed with her parents and only when Junaid finally managed to get permanent work for which he was qualified, did Humera feel relieved.

The one thing remaining was the matter of their tickets to London. Junaid had been sending money regularly for his family as soon as he had the job. He was the oldest son and had to look after his mother, younger brothers and sisters who were still at school and needed support. After working for a whole month, Junaid wrote to Humera about the system of weekly wages there and that he received twenty-one pounds every week. Humera quickly converted these pounds into rupees and it appeared to her that Junaid's monthly salary came to three thousand rupees. She was overjoyed, because his monthly earnings in India were only three hundred rupees, which was not sufficient for the whole family to live on. When Junaid started working, he found a job in Hyderabad, where everything was dearer than his home-town —

as they usually are in the big cities. His family lived in Aurangabad, so he had to support two families.

Humera would often ask him about life in London. Once Junaid wrote the prices of butter, eggs and bread. These items were quite expensive in India and only those with money could include them in their diet. The lower middle class people could not afford these items for their daily meals. When Humera converted these prices into rupees she was satisfied that they too could afford them now.

After two years' savings Junaid was able to buy the tickets for his family. Humera went to Aurangabad to meet her in-laws and told them not to worry. They would continue receiving money regularly. She cared about her mother and sisters-in-law. She was very compassionate towards Junaid's mother, who had spent her life in hunger and poverty.

When Humera arrived at London's Heathrow airport, she had to pinch herself to be sure that she was not dreaming. She had dreamt of it so often! So many of her friends had already come to London, but she could not do so. A few of them had got married and had come with their husbands. She would observe that and despair in her heart about her own situation. Within a week after arriving in England, Humera had converted everything from shillings to rupees (in those days the prices were in shillings, pence and pounds). Seeing these prices she lost every hope of becoming rich. Within a couple of months, when she did the housekeeping and paid for gas, electricity, rent and coal bills, she had spent all of her housekeeping money. Instead of saving any, she had to spend the children's allowances as well. In that period she also became aware that they had only one identity in this country: they were classified as 'blacks'. They were nothing else, not even human, and this belief was presented and supported in every way. To make matters worse, the newspapers too enhanced this opinion and demonstrated it enthusiastically and diligently. This showed that the British, with all their claims of being civilised, sophisticated and humane were, in reality, quite racist.

Humera joined evening classes soon after her arrival in England. She wanted to improve her English so that she could do some course or have training of some kind. If she could find work, perhaps their financial position might improve. She could attend these only for a few weeks because she became pregnant, although she had been very careful not to have any more children. When her fourth child was born, she could not buy anything for the baby and went to hospital empty-handed. The baby had to use the hospital's clothes. She and the baby had to stay there longer because both were very weak. During that period she received the maternity allowance and Junaid bought a few clothes for the baby. The baby's clothes were so expensive that she was amazed by their high prices. She couldn't afford to buy a pram, a bathtub, or any woollies. When she came home she used the bathroom wash-basin to bathe the baby. When she had to go to the clinic, she carried the baby in her arms. There were other women from India and Pakistan who also came to that clinic.

One day the nurse from the clinic, when alone, explained to her, "Winter will be here soon and you never know when it might snow. Your child is growing now so you ought to buy a pram, dear. The child would be safe in the pram, you can't go on with your Indian tradition here and carry the baby in your arms. Look how sensible those women are. They are also from India, Pakistan and Bangladesh and they had bought everything before the birth of their child, as women do in this country." While Humera was listening to that 'advice', she remembered her own childhood. Her mother had sent for a pram for her from Bombay, because in those days you could not buy these goods in Hyderabad. There was a servant in the house who took her out every morning and evening in her pram to the garden.

After listening to the nurse, she replied indignantly, "Please don't tell me how to look after my child properly. Twenty-eight years ago my parents brought me up the way you are telling me to. What can I do if I cannot afford these things? I wonder why I came here, because I have found nothing in this country." After that she started crying and became hysterical. The nurse was embarrassed and, putting her arms around Humera's shoulders, she comforted her and apologised.

After her son's birth Humera started studying English at home. Her teacher came once a week. It was difficult studying at home, and when she had her lessons she would leave her four children in one room, because the winter had started and she could heat only one room. Although they had three bedrooms, it was a problem to keep them warm, so they had to sleep in one room to save the heating costs. Children are meant to be noisy and troublesome and often the youngest would wake up during her lesson and start crying. Then the others would start running around and making a noise. This would distract Humera from her studies and often she would not understand what the teacher was telling her. Somehow the time would pass and the lesson would come to an end. Then the youngest child became sick and so, with him and the house work, it became too much for her. So much so, that her studies came to an end.

As time went by, instead of getting used to London, Humera became tired of her life. There was nothing there for her except work all day long — housework and the children's work. She could feel the stark similarities between Hyderabad and London. Her life pattern was the same, she had nothing there and did not possess anything worth having here either. She made no friends in her own community, because she felt her house was not as nicely decorated as theirs. They had children too and also the fact that only their husbands were working made her even more depressed. Her house, which always looked like the proverbial Indian widow, was deprived of any ornament or beautiful things. It made her very aware of her financial situation. Humera gave up every hope of doing any study or obtaining any training.

When her youngest child attended school she went to the Employment Exchange and, with a letter from them, she went looking for work in a factory. The factory manager saw the letter and showed her around. Then he gave her a form and told her to start work from the next day. There were a lot of machines there and how very strange they were!

Humera had six months' paid training and she was happy with her work. She was the only non-white worker among four hundred

women. Those working with her belonged to all walks of life. The older women usually came from well-off families whose husbands had good jobs. They were only working to save money for holidays or Christmas. The girls and the young women had mixed backgrounds. Some of them were quite illiterate even after spending twelve years in school. During the working hours these women enjoyed vulgar jokes. They talked of clothes, fashion and pub gossip while Humera would keep herself busy at her work. One day, when one of the women was chatting with a machine fitter about a very obscene and sexual matter, the other women laughed aloud listening to her. Then someone asked Humera a question concerning the same subject. She couldn't speak and went red with embarrassment. So the woman said, "Humera understands everything, she is fooling us. If she can't understand, then why is she blushing?" Some of these women despised Humera. A woman, who was transferred from a different section, had a grudge against her for no reason. Her husband had lost his job and she would taunt Humera: "These bloody blacks are taking our jobs. Bloody foreigners!" One day at lunch time, when she was in the canteen, a woman sitting next to her asked, "You are used to eating while squatting on the floor; how do you feel sitting down like this? Do you have a table and chairs at home?"

Once she had to oil some part of a machine before assembling it thoroughly. Her nose itched with the foul smell of the oil. Since her hands weren't free, she scratched it with the sleeves of her overall. When another woman saw her doing that, she offered her a tissue saying; "Use this love, don't clean your nose with the overall." Humera became very angry but didn't know what to say and how to say it. Then someone spoke out in protest on her behalf. She did have some friends!

One day she was talking to a woman and she made some complaints about her house. Listening to her conversation, someone made a malicious comment, "You ought to be grateful that you are in this country. You used to live in a hut in India, didn't you?"

These women knew only what they had seen on television. They believed that all Indians were beggars. All the time Humera had been in England, the television showed the same picture of India. Only when there was an interview with Mrs. Indira Gandhi, would things look nice and elegant. Otherwise there was nothing but squalor. Every time they showed that country, it would be the same rubbish dumps and snivelling, naked children! Every scene would have cows and mangy dogs, and children sleeping next to them. In these scenes, more often than not, there would be a poor woman making cow-dung cakes and flies swarming everywhere.

One day Humera's six-year-old daughter came home from school crying because her schoolmates had been asking her a lot of hurtful questions. They had asked her: "How did you travel from India? Did you walk or come by ox-cart?" When she told them that they had come by aeroplane, they did not believe her. They said that she was lying because they have seen it on TV and women there always put their belonging on their heads when they travel. "Did you do that, carry your things on your head? Indians always travel by ox-cart. You must have done that."

Sometimes Humera would be fed up with everything and feel a sudden urge to go back home. If she had to suffer the same fate as she had back there, what was the point of this hard life? Apart from anything else, she felt sad that she could not send as much money to her in-laws as she wanted to. Neither she nor her husband could afford to send any more money to make their families live any better. If she went back home she would certainly be closer to her parents, but what was her role in India as a Muslim now? It was more distressing to see how the Muslims were treated in India. Although they, too, were Indians, now they were regarded as foreigners in their own country. She had been through that racism in India. She knew she was labelled as a 'black' here in England, but in India she was branded as Muslim. She often worried that her children were not learning their mother tongue and were ignorant about their culture and religious education. But what kind of future would they have in India? They would neither learn their mother tongue nor anything about their religion. What they read in school would be about the Hindu religion, only about Ram and Krishna. Indian culture and its values had changed a great deal. At other times she would seriously consider the possibility of going back. She felt that if she went home with the children, then the money spent there would give them a better life in India and help her mother-in-law. But she knew that she would never do that. The children had missed their father so much, when he had come to England and they were back home, waiting for their tickets. It would not be a good thing for their upbringing if they were separated from their father. And so, she did find some ray of hope in remaining in England. At least the children would be able to get a better education and her children's educational records, so far, had been excellent. They were always ahead of their age group. One has to make some compromises in life, Humera believed, and she had to do the same. She would try to be happy with what she had in life!

(The title of the story in Urdu is *Halat Se Samjhota*.)

FIROZA JAFFER

THE LUNCHEON CLUB

Firoza Jaffer *is from Karachi where she obtained her Master's degree in literature. She came to London in 1968 and did a diploma in Adult Education. She writes poetry, short stories and essays. Her works have been widely published in Pakistan and the UK. A collection of her short stories has come out. She is also an eloquent speaker and generally speaks on religion and social matters. She teaches English and Urdu in the College of North-East London and lives in London.*

It has been about two years since the Social Centre was established in this area and ever since, there was always something going on. Sometimes, it was the festival of *Holi,* at others, there would be a jumbo sale being organised on a grand scale. At the festival of *Diwali,* there was a lot of hustle and bustle, and the upstairs hall was decorated with colourful buntings and sweet melodies filled the place. Then it was heard that a luncheon club, for the old people was going to be opened in the Centre. Also, that there would be food available at a reduced rate and it would open every day of the week, except Sunday.

Soon after that people were being selected to run the Luncheon Club. Then, one Saturday afternoon, the Luncheon Club was inaugurated and there were cameras being clicked and photographs taken. Hot and freshly fried *poori* with spicy *tarkari* were served for the guests. Their flavour, mingled with the aroma of piping hot, sweet *halwa*, was enough to make anyone ravenous. Among those present were the Centre's employees and those willing to do voluntary work. Next day, the local newspapers had prominently published the photos of the Centre's workers, avidly eating *halwa poori* and *aaloo-chhole.*

The Club started to run smoothly and was very busy all the time. Although lunch time was at one o'clock, people would start coming at about ten or eleven. These old people, dressed in heavy coats, with caps and scarves, and thick glasses, would come there with a certain eagerness. The women came too, attired in saris or *salwar* suits and coats. There were some women who did not like to take their coats off because there were men around. Some would cover their head with their sari, others would keep their scarves on. At first they started speaking to each other in hushed tones, gradually their voices became normal, as they got used to each other and became friends. Then the time came when they no longer felt like strangers with each other. The conversation started departing from the changing weather and extended to everyday ailments. Along with arthritis and progressing cataracts, family matters were discussed. They talked about old memories and stories from the past, and the things they remembered most. In the beginning, the women used to sit separately, but slowly the groups of men and women blended, and they began to sit together. Hushed tone altered to a normal pitch as conversation proceeded. Though still somewhat hesitant, they began to talk about their lives and personal matters too: "I don't know what my daughter-in-law said to my son, but he was being very difficult this morning," Osha Bai craned her neck and addressed Premji.

"My back pain kept me awake all night. It was very late and I couldn't sleep, I just had the lights on, to take my tablets, when I heard my son-in-law complaining to Asha — my daughter. He was telling her, 'It is because of your father that our electricity bill has been going up all the time. He always has the lights on.'"

Premji spoke of his own troubles, "Oh, it is a daily routine to blame me — they always do! When the central heating is off and I switch the heater on for a moment just to warm my toes, my daughter-in-law goes mad." Ayesha Begum grabbed the opportunity to present her own case, "If I want to hold my grandson for a while and play with him, she says, 'Do not spoil him!' As if I had spoiled her husband!" She looked around her, seeking justice.

The early indifference slowly began to disappear. The lunch was just an excuse really, they enjoyed the get-together. Going to the Centre was like an outing. It was closed on Sundays, but when it opened on Monday, these old people would enter the club with the enthusiasm of a child who has found his lost toy. During the winter season more people visited the Centre. Probably the central heating system in their homes was timed very accurately. So, to avoid the cold, they would come here. They would sit in the warm and comfortable hall of the Centre, sip their tea or play cards. Sometimes they would go to the Reading Room and read the newspapers, old or new, in their own mother tongues. Some would just sit and watch what was going on around them. Among those quiet people was Malti Ben, who was suffering from terrible knee pain. The doctor had told her that when the cold penetrates the bones, the pain gets worse and in old age it becomes severe. Malti Ben took endless tablets and capsules but nothing helped to ease the pain. She lived a long way from the Centre. Someone had told her about it and one day, when she went to the hospital, she got off near the Centre. Asking for directions, she found it. She was surprised to see that the people gathered there were just like her — unhappy and lonely old people who were cut off from real life, and the joys of life. "What did I come here for?" she asked herself.

"The social worker came to see me. She told me that a wheel chair would be available next month," a weak voice rose from a corner. Malti Ben felt like a cinema-goer who goes to the pictures to enjoy herself, but finds the film making her even sadder and comes back with a heavy heart. She stood there by the door. No one looked at her or asked her anything. They didn't even ask her to sit down. Malti Ben regretted coming. Suddenly the pain in her knees shot through like an electric current and it made her whole body tremble. She placed her hand on the wall for support and slowly tried to move forward. She made an unsuccessful attempt to sit on the high stool she saw before her, then staggered and bumped into someone. Tears of frustration filled her eyes, everything became even more hazy. Then somebody held her hand and made her sit down in an armchair. She wiped her face and looked at the person who had helped her. The gentleman had dark glasses on and his face was expressionless. Perhaps he did not know that if he hadn't helped Malti Ben, she would have fallen on the floor. Malti Ben thanked him in a low voice. Only after listening to her did he realise that it was a woman he had helped.

"I can't see properly — sorry I would not have touched you," he was embarrassed. Malti Ben wanted to say that she had come to the Centre to enjoy herself a little — but there was so much pain everywhere. Instead she spoke in a muffled voice, "Somebody told me that lots of people come here. I thought I might meet someone I know. But I don't see anyone here..." she was looking around with disappointment.

"My name is Khan... Saeed Khan. I live nearby. I can't see properly. When people see my white cane they help me. I get here somehow. You come here and you are bound to get to know others." He was trying to put her at ease. Malti Ben wanted to ask,

"Aren't you afraid to come out of the house? The cars go so fast that I am frightened to put a foot down on the road." But she couldn't ask anything. She just rubbed her swelling knees and looked at Khan Saheb. They were both sitting near the door. Someone brought two cups of hot tea for them. Khan Saheb took a sip, "Oh, no sugar — and when it is our turn to get the sugar the tea will be ice cold." Malti Ben holding the arms of the chair stood up. "I'll get the sugar. I can't drink tea without sugar".

When tea was finished the clock chimed four. The afternoon light was disappearing and it was getting dark. People were getting ready to go home, hurriedly putting their coats, scarves and caps on. Malti Ben hadn't taken her coat off. She bent down to pick up her medicine bag from the floor and spoke to herself, "Oh *Bhagwan*, Oh Lord, let it not rain tomorrow." Hidden in this one sentence were perhaps her thanks and goodbye to Khan Saheb — and also a desire to visit the Centre the next day.

The Luncheon Club had only one kind of menu, a vegetarian one; rice, lentils, *poori* and *tarkari,* and different kinds of pickles and chutneys. There was always a sweet dish. People who came here weren't all vegetarians. Some of them ate fish and meat. Still, when they were served this inexpensive steaming hot lunch, some people had already forgotten that they did not like vegetables. At home, if they missed meat for even two days in a row, they would get so cross that their blood pressure would rise, creating tension during meal times. However, having their lunch at the Centre and eating on disposable plates, they did not actually think about the food, or its taste. Perhaps being together made them happy. They felt as if they had their family around them and enjoyed the warmth and closeness.

Mirza Saheb had to come a long way. His next door neighbour's daughter, who was English, would sometimes drop him there in her car. He couldn't stop saying how kind she was! Mirza Saheb's daughter-in-law had taken his pension book and kept it. Now she wanted him to go and live in an old people's home. But his son wouldn't hear of it!

"Papa is always coughing — our little Bobby gets frightened during his sleep in the night." When she saw that her husband wasn't very attentive to her complaints, she started bringing up these excuses. "I don't have any time to rest. There's the house work and Papa has so many phone calls — and your son wakes me up so often at night. How can he sleep, poor thing, when his grandfather keeps coughing and clearing his throat?" Mirza Saheb's son could have gone on listening to his wife's complaints until they affected his darling son's health. "If he is disturbed all the time, it'll affect his growth," she said. Putting aside his filial emotions, he had to make a decision about his father. Quietly, he contacted an old people's home and arranged for Mirza Saheb to be admitted there.

When Mirza Saheb got some inkling about this arrangement, he was dumb founded. Iqbal was his only son. His wife had died young of breast cancer when the boy was only five years old. He didn't get married again because he did not wish for Iqbal to have a stepmother who would make him suffer. He had a stepmother and had had a terrible childhood. He couldn't even bear to think that any harm should come to his son. He was a guard on British Rail and had retired from the same job. In his working days, he had shift duties, but he never let his son feel his mother's absence. Whether he had to go to work early in the morning when there were still stars in the sky, or in the freezing winter afternoon, he had only one thing in his mind, "Iqbal must be looked after properly." There was only one aim in his life, that his son shouldn't feel deprived or become unhappy. They started talking openly about Mirza Saheb going to a 'Home'. The day and dates were being fixed. Mirza Saheb was sure of it and he raised hell. He shouted and screamed at his son and daughter-in-law and told them some home truths. He told his son what he had done for him and threatened to call the radio and television people and give them an interview. He was going to tell them about his son's behaviour. Then, through the Social Services he arranged for a Home Help.

"My daughter-in-law, Nasreen — she was taking an allowance from the Social Security. She was getting the money because she claimed she was looking after me, full time!" Mirza Saheb was sitting in the Centre, telling the story of his life to all and sundry. He wasn't at all embarrassed about divulging details of his family life. Thirty years ago, he had arrived in England carrying a little boy. He had immigrated thinking that he might be able to make a better future for his son. He had experienced a lot of heartaches in the process of settling in a new country. But his son's present, and perhaps future, life were secured. The father who had abandoned his own security and his own roots was now recounting what was happening to him and the home he had worked so hard to make. He was sitting in the Centre and the book of his life was open for everyone to read. His life had been full of loneliness, responsibilities and long hours at work. Now he was pleading with them to give him the justice he really deserved.

Every day Malti Ben would listen to a new story. As she got to know the people she began to like the Centre more. She was married into an orthodox Hindu family, and was very careful not to be physically touched by others. She was very cautious about her food and avoided garlic and onion altogether, as she was required to do by orthodox dietary rules. When she started going to the Centre, she wouldn't take any refreshment all day except tea. When she saw that women of her own caste and from similar orthodox families like hers were enjoying the platefuls of freshly fried *poori* and *tarkari,* slowly she began to relent and think that maybe she didn't have to forego the food either.

One day, with great courage, she picked up a plate and put a little rice and *dal* with *saag* — pulses and greens — and started eating a tiny mouthful. The smell of garlic and onion being fried in the kitchen would waft in the hall, but now it didn't matter to her. There were many Hindus, Muslims and Sikhs sitting at the same table, eating and drinking together from similar plates and cups. They all looked the same and they all had the same heads with the silvery grey streaks, the same kind of wrinkles on their cheeks and brows. "How do we know who was different from whom, and why so many restrictions? God knows who started them?" Fed up, she closed her eyes.

Sakina Begum was one of those women who came to the Centre quite regularly. She was an awe-inspiring lady. When Idi Amin ordered the Asians (who were settled in Uganda for generations) to leave the country, she came to England with her five children. Her only daughter was already married to someone from her own family. Her four sons were married after settling in England. Sakina Begum was a sharp-tongued woman who never got on with any of her daughters-in-law. She was always threatening to leave them and go and live with her daughter. Her son-in-law wasn't very happy with her either. So her daughter couldn't keep her mother in her home and take the risk of offending her husband.

Sakina Begum was from the northern part of India called UP. When she got married, she went to Kampala. The English language was very common in East African countries. Sakina Begum had lived there for thirty long years and learned a few English words. When she came to London, she started attending Neighbourhood Classes for English. She was not only sharp-tongued but also quite intelligent and learned enough English to read and write quickly. She liked to discuss politics, and now she was more interested in current affairs which she discussed at all times. Compared to Idi Amin, the British were like God for Sakina Begum who wouldn't hear anything against them.

"They have given you asylum, haven't they? If they throw you out, what will happen then?" The hall would reverberate with her loud voice. Every time a new daughter-in-law was brought home, Sakina was sure to have petty arguments and rows with her. When family matters went from bad to worse, she gave them an ultimatum — she would leave home! At the beginning, her sons and their wives believed it to be just an empty threat. Since she had settled in London, Sakina Begum had got to know the rules and regulations of this country as well. And she knew her rights too. She went to the Citizens Advice Bureau, told them her story in a moving way and asked for their help. She got a council flat and now she lived there alone. She was very pleased that she was using all the facilities available in this country.

"I live the way I want. Nobody dares to interfere with my life!" Sakina Begum would spread her legs sitting in the armchair and show off her independence. The fact that she was not living with her sons and that they were being criticised by their community for not looking after their old mother, was also a source of no mean satisfaction to her.

"She is too old to live alone, in a foreign country and nobody to look after her!" People would comment gravely.

"Oh, she is a cantankerous old woman herself — she couldn't live with any of them, she can't! You can blame one son and his wife — but all of them could never be as bad as she claims!" Razia Khatoon would speak irritatedly. She could never get on with Sakina Begum. She had come from a far away village in Punjab and could not even speak Urdu properly, so there was no question of her knowing any English. Sometimes she would come to the Centre with her husband. Razia had never had any children and listening to these old parents' complaining about their children, her pain for not having any was gradually fading.

All the religious festivals were celebrated at the Centre with equal pomp and splendour. This year they had a great celebration at *Baisakhi* and *Holi*. At *Diwali,* they had an evening of singing and dancing. All Club members worked with the Centre's employees and arranged everything splendidly and cooked all kinds of special dishes. It was the same at Christmas.

Father Christmas stood at the door of the Centre, the hall was decorated with colourful buntings and balloons. English people, who worked for the council, were also invited for the party. A traditional Christmas cake was cut and people gave each other presents, wrapped in flowery-patterned, shiny-coloured paper. Presents were exchanged with great cheerfulness and people showed each other their gifts. They had left so much happiness behind in their homeland. Outside the Centre there was the hustle and bustle of life and it was full of activity. Everyone was busy and lost in his own world. Those immersed in this fast flow of time did not have a moment to stop and look at people whose life resembled still water, dull and dreary, with nothing to look forward to. Who would want to stop for a moment and think about them? Those who came to the Centre were people who had spent all their active life working and building a future for their families. The women, who had children, had spent their entire lives looking after them. They had never thought about themselves and their own desires. They had reserved all their hopes and longing for their children — who were a part of them, their own flesh and blood. Their children were their hopes, aspirations and destiny. They had dreamed about the bright shiny future which belonged to their children. But now they were no longer a part of that future. By the time these tired and weary people realised this, things had already changed so much. Even the air they breathed felt different. Their life was like some strange confusion which had spread everywhere. Their hopes were now like clattering shackles which had wounded their dreams. Life had become useless to an extent they had never anticipated. In such circumstances, the Luncheon Club was a refuge for these lonely souls who were cut off from life. Here, they found solace. It brought them together for just a short period of time, yet the friendship and shared moments gave them immense pleasure. Here they became active and felt alive. Never mind the fact that these people were just acquaintances, not family.

Eid was coming soon, and an *Eid Milan* party was being organised. The Centre had begun to play an important role in Malti Ben's insipid life. She had, to a certain extent, gained confidence and was no longer shy and diffident. She was now taking part in many of the activities in the Centre. When *Raksha- Bandhan* came, she brought many *bandhans,* made of shiny colourful threads and tied them to many people's wrists. On every festival, they felt happy as if their childhood had returned. They would be excited like children — anguish and bitterness being pushed to the back of their mind. Malti Ben was thinking about the *Eid*s of her childhood days. In her home-town, Ahmedabad, she always went to her Muslim neighbour's house on the morning of *Eid* to pay her respects to the lady of the house, whom her mother, *Mataji* (mother), had taught her to call Fatima *Khala* or Fatima aunty.

She would place a silver coin in Malti Ben's little hand and give her blessings, "*Eid Mubarak* — may God bless you, my dear." Then she would call out to her children, "Saleem, see who is here. Salma — bring some hot vermicelli for Malti *beti.*"

For years, Malti Ben had cooked the same sweet vermicelli like Fatima *Khala* with zest. She now carefully carried the bowl of

vermicelli, which was flavoured with *kewda* water and thin flakes of almonds and pistachio spread all over. She was wearing the new grey sari that her daughter-in-law had bought for her the previous year. She had thrown the packet in front of Malti Ben and remarked scornfully, "Now saris are getting very expensive, you ought to wear trousers. A couple of trousers will see you through the whole year," and Malti Ben's face had turned pale grey, like the colour of the old and worn-out sari she was wearing. "Everybody is wearing them here — and you also have pain in your knees. You cannot even use the Hoover." How could the daughter-in-law see the misery in Malti Ben's pale face? After that Malti Ben had begun hoovering the house somehow. She had stopped asking her daughter-in-law to go to the hospital or to the doctor's with her. No matter how sharp-tongued Sakina Begum was, she was a great help to Malti Ben. She had taken the responsibility of going to hospital with her and explaining everything to the doctors and nurses in English and telling them all her problems, the growing pain in her knees.

"Why have you cooked this rich sweet dish, and why this new sari?" The daughter-in-law had come home for lunch.

"It is *Eid* today — I'm taking it to the Centre," she replied, speaking in a low voice.

"Oh! So you have cooked this for that blind old Pakistani — the man you were helping to cross the road the other day. Don't you feel ashamed — *Pitaji* (father) has been dead for twenty long years — and now you...!"

Malti Ben could not hear any more. What was this smell, where was it coming from? She had scrubbed the house clean to the extent that her hands were all rough and the skin had come off. Then what was this foul smell — as if somebody had emptied the rubbish bin inside the kitchen. A feeling of nausea came over her. She closed her eyes and the sweet smelling bowl of rich vermicelli fell on the floor and broke into pieces. She realised that it wasn't only her knees that were hurting her, her hands too had no strength left in them.

(The story has the same title in Urdu.)

MOHSINA JILANI

THE GOLDEN CAGE

Mohsina Jilani *is from Pakistan. She did her graduation from Muslim University, Aligarh, and* Munshi Kamil, *a high standard Urdu language exam, from Allahabad University. She obtained a teaching diploma in London, and taught Urdu and Arabic in North London. She wrote a column for women in London's Urdu daily,* Jang, *and also the* London Letter *in a Pakistani newspaper, Lahore. Mohsina regularly took part in the Women's Programme of the BBC Urdu Service, and works in the Audience Research Unit of the BBC World Service. She is one of the founders of the first literary organisation for women writers of the Urdu language. She writes poetry and short stories which have been widely published in Pakistan, India and UK. She lives in London.*

A blast of icy wind froze her, but wrapping her pink *dupatta* around her head, she kept on walking, hastening her pace. Where could she go? That question had left her with a feeling of total helplessness. She saw a telephone booth ahead, thought of using it, but knew she could not. When she didn't even know how to use a telephone or how to dial a number, how was she going to contact the police? She did not know the language either, how was she going to say anything to them at all?

She didn't even know the name of the road she was walking on, knew no one and nobody would recognise her. She had been in London for only six months and she did not know either the language or what to make of its weather. That's why she had left the house in her thin *salwar kameez*, without even a coat.

Even if she could speak to them, what was she going to tell the police anyway? Thinking about this, a flood of tears once again drenched her face. *Oh Amma! Oh dear mother! Where have you sent me? What kind of country did you marry me into and what sort of people are these two, the father and the son*?

She could still hear the voice of her old father-in-law, echoing in her ears, saying, "We share everything in this house, almost everything. My son doesn't come here anymore. It seems he's got married to his girlfriend, and now you are going to sleep in my room." The words 'in my room' echoed and she covered her ears with her hands. She could not bear any more and burst out crying. He had insinuated it often enough, but today his attitude was different. Behind the face of that old man, she saw the devil peeping through.

Taj Bibi had begun to sweat with fear. Quickly she had served the food to the old man and run to the kitchen. She wanted to take something to go to sleep forever. Within six months of her married life she had been through hell. Every Friday evening, Khairuddin would enter the house quietly. He would carry large cardboard boxes of groceries and fruit and vegetables and drop them loudly on the kitchen floor. Then his father, collecting the money from him, would frown and complain, "Why have you nothing to do with this house now? Not even with the woman you

have brought and left here only to exist. Why don't you send her back to her village?" While counting the money Khairuddin would stop, then placing the money on his father's palm he would smile, "What's the problem? She is looking after you, isn't she?" His English girlfriend, sitting in the grocery van outside, would blow the horn and Khairuddin would jump up to go to her.

The old man knew very well that this was Khairuddin's girlfriend. She knew about his wife being in the house now, yet she had kept her hold on him. Taj Bibi had felt as if Khairuddin had walked all over her. She used to have some hope that her husband might come back to her one day.

That evening she was shaken so badly that it felt as if an earthquake had hit her. "You sleep in my bedroom tonight—remember, in my bedroom, we share everything here."

She was feeling hot as if the blood in her body had rushed to her head and that her brain was about to explode. Quietly, she came out of the kitchen, gingerly opened the door and without making the slightest noise went through the hallway, hurriedly opened the front door and started running down the road as fast as she could. *What kind of a man was he*? The thought rushed through her mind, that she had treated him like a father, and he had behaved in such an uncouth manner. Whenever he had hit her, she had always kept quiet.

"What sort of place is this? Oh fate, what world have you thrown me into?"

The night was getting dark, and covered in the mist, the flickering red, amber streetlights of the city had become even more hazy. The fog was so thick that she couldn't see more than a couple of yards ahead. She was frightened and moved to one side. Now she was slowing down. She didn't know the city and had no relations in London to go to.

When she came to this country from the free and open atmosphere of her village she had had the feeling that she was now kept in a beautiful golden cage, where she had all the material comforts and food but no one to speak to, no one who would listen to what she wanted to say. The old man spent all day in front of the television. Khairuddin worked in a grocery store, and his girlfriend was also employed there. Taj Bibi had become aware of her husband's extra-marital affair, the first day that she had set foot in London. She had been married through the telephone, a marriage by proxy. As she had been paid five thousand rupees, her mother did not think it was a bad bargain. There were four daughters to marry, and Taj Bibi was the eldest one. Taj Bibi could still smell the perfume she wore on her wedding day. The scent would sometimes still waft around her. The real reason why this marriage took place was that the father and son needed a woman just to look after the house, and cook and clean for them — that was all!

Everything in the house was a novelty for her. She would look at every item with amazement, and her eyes opened wide in astonishment; gas cooker, the washing machine, the vacuum cleaner. You just pressed a button and all the work was done. It was a world full of wonder, a very different one from her own. In her mother's house all the doors were broken and not one could be properly secured. But how safe she had felt there! She had her mother's and sisters' shoulders to cry on, to share her joys and sorrows. She was happy with simple things and life had not been so bad, had it? Her village, where night began when the stars twinkled in the sky and morning came with the first rays of the sun. Her village was so dear to her even with all its poverty and deprivation. Here she had all the home comforts, secure doors, yet how insecure she felt! She had no one to turn to in this desperate situation.

Taj Bibi started walking fast again, sweating in the cold freezing wind. Where was she going? What was her destination? What door was she going to knock? She knew nothing. After about a mile she saw a bus stop and stopped. It was a little peaceful at the bus shelter. There were a few people waiting for the bus; they now looked at her with curiosity. What kind of girl was she? Running around without a coat and clad probably in her night clothes. They seemed to be aware of her distressed condition, but the traditional English habit of non-interference led them to keep quiet. The bus came, its automatic doors opened, people got on but Taj Bibi's feet were clamped to the ground. She didn't have a single coin for the fare and where would she go? Perhaps she was going to stay at the bus stop all night and freeze in this weather. Her dead body would be lying there in the morning. The thought of death made her tremble. She wanted to ask people for help but she was frightened of them. When the bus left she relaxed a little, now she was able to think things out.

How nice it would be if she were to die there — right then, but the thought of death wasn't a very pleasant one, and it made her shiver. She longed for someone to hold her hand and ask her, "Why do you wish to die so young? Why have you run away from home? Look at the night of London city, so brilliantly illuminated. See, those two people seem to be in love — the way they are whispering to each other. The shining cars moving fast on the gleaming road; the dark sky and far-away lights sparkling and flickering, just like your hopes. London is so beautiful at night." But nobody asked her anything and she kept wondering what to do in her anguished state of mind. She could see something coming in front of her. Taj Bibi kept remembering all the people of her village one by one. That old woman who was very helpful and loving and everyone called her *Amma*. How nice she was! Whenever there was a wedding in the village, she would always help. If there was a quarrel between a husband and wife, or between a daughter and mother-in-law, that good woman would be there to mediate, to help to resolve the matter and to provide comfort. In Taj Bibi's own wedding, she had been in the forefront.

She wished for a miracle to happen and prayed that when the next bus came and its doors opened she would see *Amma* getting down. She would cuddle up to her bosom and weep her heart out. There wasn't a bus for a long time. That must have been the last one. The night was slipping away, and there were very few cars now. Every moment was becoming darker for Taj Bibi and she was beginning to feel frightened. Now and then the noise of a moving ambulance would break the silence of the night and her heart would be in her mouth with fear. A little while ago she had wanted to die, now she was terrified of it. If any car or bus were to come along she would surely ask for help. If she could not speak English, then she could use sign language. Several cars came and roared by but Taj Bibi stood there. Suddenly, she saw a taxi coming fast. Panicked, and not knowing what to do, she ran and stood in the middle of the road. The taxi had been going at full speed and the driver just managed to stop in front of her. The brakes made such a sound that she was even more frightened. The driver of the taxi hurriedly opened the door and came out to enquire, and looking at her standing there he became very angry. He got hold of her shoulders and shook her roughly, "What do you think you are doing? Do you want to die, lady? But why did you choose to die in front of my taxi, why? You could have had me killed too — you know that? You crazy girl!"

Taj Bibi's blood froze and her breathing made a hissing sound. The taxi driver had roughly gripped her shoulders and then suddenly he released her. Taj Bibi was a picture of innocence; the golden button on her *kurta,* shone and its pink colour lit up in the bright light. He was dazzled by the sight, his voice softened as he asked, "Why do you want to die, love?

"Can you speak English?

"Where is your home?

"Shall I take you home?"

Taj Bibi stood there like a statue, she had lost all her senses. All her married life she had never heard such a sweet and softly spoken man's voice. She looked up with her angelic face and saw that kind man, with intent blue eyes and a kind face. For a moment, she was neither Asian nor Western, Indian nor Pakistani — she was just a woman — a woman who was helpless, in need of a friend. She could not speak but she had a heart full of emotions and longing and there he was — this man standing in front of her, tall and strong and concerned. Suddenly, she placed her head on his chest and started to cry bitterly, as if she had found her security for life. He was patting her shoulders with such sympathy and tenderness, that she knew he was trying to comfort her. Gently, he moved her from his chest. Then taking his jacket from the back seat of the taxi, he wrapped it around shivering Taj Bibi's shoulders. Then, with great respect and care, he opened the front door of the taxi and helped her inside. Taj Bibi was still crying.

"Now, where shall I take you?" he asked her, knowing that she would not be able to understand him. He spoke as if he was talking to himself. "Shall I take you to the Police Station or to the refuge for runaway girls? It is better that we go to the Police Station," he was trying to tell her. "I don't know what has happened to you, and I am sorry that I don't know your language. But don't worry, dear, you are quite safe with me. Nobody can touch you now."

In between her sobs, Taj Bibi had been silently pleading with him, "Take me to your home. I will clean your house and cook for you and look after you. I do not want anything in return, nothing. But for God's sake don't take me to Khairuddin, please, please don't take me back to him!"

(The title of the story in Urdu is *Soney Ka Pinjra.*)

PERVEEN MIRZA

FLAMES AND FEALTY

Perveen Mirza *comes from Karachi, Pakistan. She obtained her degree from Karachi University, and came to London after her marriage. She worked for the BBC Urdu Service, and the BBC Television programme for Asians. Afterwards, she worked for Asian TV and Radio Stations, presenting and producing programmes for Asian listeners. Her voice is well known to both listeners and viewers of the Asian community. Perveen writes short stories and poetry, which have been published in the UK and Pakistan. She lives in London.*

It was a sunny and bright morning as is seldom seen in London. She was restless today and could not do any work. She felt as if a needle had pierced through her heart. The breakfast dishes were still in the kitchen unwashed, and the onions were getting brown in the pot on the cooker. It was a Sunday morning but she hadn't finished any of her kitchen chores yet. How could she go to the garden, where Farooq, with his garden tools, had been for a long time. She knew very well that to enjoy the weather fully her next door neighbour, Mrs. Jones, wearing a bikini, would be sunbathing in her easy-chair. Her body would be smeared with suntan lotion. She also knew that today Farooq would be there in the garden till late afternoon. He would look at Mrs. Jones through the green netting fence. Then he would smile first and say good morning. After a little while he would make general comments about the flowers and the weather. In this way he would successfully start a conversation with her, and being a passionate gardener, she would not be able to resist the temptation to get up and move closer. She would approve of the flower beds he had dug and the flowers he had planted.

Then, shaking the mud off his hands, he would get up and standing very close to her, he would chat for hours. Mrs. Jones, with her smooth, creamy white skin would be standing just opposite to him, and the thin netting fence would be the only partition between them. She felt like rolling up her sleeves and going out to the garden and challenging her.

"Could you find only my husband to show your naked body?" But how could she say it all. How could she speak to Mrs. Jones? Her limited vocabulary of English would fail her when compared to Mrs. Jones' native fluency.

Back home she had obtained a BA degree, and how proud *Amma*, her mother, was. How *Amma* had kept repeating this fact to her in-laws when they had come to ask for her hand in marriage. Now it felt as if she had no education at all and that she had wasted her time, as she was neither able to understand nor speak any English now, in the way it was spoken. In order to learn to speak properly, she had joined the 'English for Foreigners' evening

class. The tube station from her house was nearby and if the weather was good she would often walk, otherwise Farooq would drive her there. There were only a few stops before the station to her college.

During her journey she would keep to herself, always trying to squeeze herself in to the pushing and shoving of the crowd. If she was pressed against someone, a man, she would look at that person with distrust and would pull herself away even more. She was careful not to let anyone touch her. How could she allow a stranger to do that, it wouldn't be proper, she was sure of it.

She could hear the laughter of Farooq and Mrs. Jones and these sounded as if molten lead had been poured into her ears. Her heart was in a turmoil again and she kept thinking: how nice Farooq was, lively and polite. Chatting with a woman, he could become exceedingly well-mannered. At times she wished she could behave rudely and holding her husband's hand, take him away. And why ever not! How irresponsible he was. As soon as he caught sight of a woman he would become totally indifferent to his wife. Ignoring her he would give all his attention to that woman. He would be polite and pleasant and behave in such a way that she would feel humiliated. While she would force a smile on her face she would burn inside with rage.

Amma married her off to a foreign land so that her daughter would be happy. Here she was, her unfortunate daughter, putting up not only with a second wife but numerous other women.

It was unusually cold that day and it was time to go for her evening classes, but she didn't feel like going out. Farooq, spread out on the sofa, was watching television. She put on her coat, and moving the curtain a little, peered outside. Draped in coats and scarves, people were walking huddled against the freezing weather. She turned towards him and said appealingly:

"Please can you take me to the station?" But he did not answer and kept watching the screen.

"Look, it's very cold today, can you take me to the station?" She almost begged.

"This weather will continue to remain cold every day. If you want to go, please manage it yourself, otherwise stay at home. I'm not going to miss this programme." His eyes remained glued on the film. She felt hurt by his answer. Then she reminded herself, *I should be used to his blunt rudeness. When he isn't in a good mood, he always reacts in this manner*. She knew very well that he would not leave the programme at any cost, and she was not sure whether she should go to her college. She was thinking about it when the door bell rang.

She opened the door and there stood Mrs. Jones, wrapped up in her woollen cap and beautiful fur coat. On her invitation, Mrs. Jones came in, and addressing Farooq she said:

"My car doesn't start and I have to go out, it's extremely important, would you...?"

He got up with a jerk as if a spring in the sofa had ejected him, and even before she had finished her sentence, he had his car keys in his hand and bowing his head smiled and said, "Certainly, certainly." Then switching the television off he said to his wife, "I will drop you off too."

She looked at her husband and his sudden alertness. Then glaring at him, she walked outside. It was very cold and a thin layer of ice covered the footpath and road, but within her the flames of anger were ablaze. Her eyes couldn't see anything, even though she was not crying. The bitterness in her thoughts and a burning anger made her feel as if her heart and soul were being scorched. She didn't know when she arrived at the station, or when she got on the train.

She had lost all awareness of things around her and she was startled when someone's knees touched hers. She looked up and saw it was a man! The man in question was oblivious to her as he was reading a newspaper. The movements of the train were making his knees brush against hers. Her entire mind was now centred on that part of her body being touched by a stranger — a man! Suddenly, an idea crossed her mind, and instead of shrinking herself into her seat she remained seated as she was. She made no move to push her leg away. She believed that this little dishonesty of hers would compensate for all of Farooq's wrongdoings. A calmness spread through her, and she felt the flames, which had been burning within her had been put out.

(The title of the story in Urdu is *Bay-Eemani.*)

FIROZE MOOKERJI

THE STORY OF SADAQAT HUSAIN KHAN

(as told by him)

Dr. Firoze Mookerji *was born near Lucknow in North India. She obtained the Master's degree from University of Lucknow, and in 1953 came to the UK to do PhD, which she did from London University under the guidance of Ralph Russell. Firoze returned to India in 1964, but came back four years later to take up a job as a teacher. She started writing at the age of fifteen, her stories and articles were published when she was still studying. But she did not write for a long time; first due to her involvement in politics and then for personal reasons. However, since her retirement from teaching in 1988, Firoze has been concentrating on her writing. Her first book,* The Critical Study of the Work of Pundit Ratan Nath Sarshar *(who is regarded as the first novelist of the Urdu language), was published in English. A collection of her short stories in Urdu is under publication. She also writes literary essays. She writes for children as well. Firoze is widely published in India, Pakistan and the UK. She lives in London.*

My name is Sadaqat Husain Khan. Sadaqat means the truth. And, by the grace of God, my name is also the true reflection of my nature. I deplore poetry and all other rubbish like that which have too many lies in them. The bright side of my personality is my truthfulness. That's why you must trust me and whatever I tell you will be nothing but the truth. These events are such that you may feel doubtful and think that they may have been fabricated. But, believe me, they have happened before my own eyes. As I have said before, I am a truthful person and I am telling you nothing but the actual facts.

As I understand it, I know that I have understood it. I am a Muslim and believe that Islam is a religion better than a lot of religious leaders and scholars (and this is not being arrogant). But the fact of the matter is that they have been, compared to me, almost like schoolchildren. I do enjoy the odd drink sometimes. Ghalib, the great poet, has written a lot of unusual things in much of his poetry. But I remember one of his couplets, in which he says: "Who drinks for pleasure? I just want to forget the pain of life."

I too drink, not because I want to derive pleasure from it, but often I need to be free from life's problems. My life sometimes does become very difficult because of my truthfulness, only then I have to have a drink. But I can claim that no harm comes to anyone from my drinking. I close the door of my room, then I open the bottle. And until my wife tires of knocking at the door I do not open it. The only reason she does it is because she wants to give me the evening meal and then retire to sleep. If it was up to her, she wouldn't do a single thing. But when I married her, I had told her on the first day that I hated laziness and indolence.

And the customary ritual of the wedding was not even finished when I sent her back to work. Her headmistress was surprised when she returned so soon after the wedding. But all women are the same, they love the wedding ceremony and all the accompanying hoo-ha about it.

It doesn't matter how much you educate them, my dear, women's natures will never change. That's why I don't have any interest in their gender. I like men, but not every Tom, Dick and

Harry. Only if I meet an educated, like-minded, sincere person who is the same age as me, then I feel very happy. Alas, seldom has this opportunity presented itself. Only once, when I went to America for postgraduate studies, did I find a friend like that. I can't tell you how handsome he was. All the girls there were infatuated with him. But he wasn't interested in them, he just liked to study, exercise for the sake of body building, and meet men of the same age and interests. He especially valued my friendship. It was as though we were two bodies with one mind. But the damned society cannot see anyone happy. God knows who had written what to my parents! In the holidays when I went back home, my father told me that I must get married and they had found a girl for me. I refused point blank. I told my father that my education wasn't finished, and I had no job. I could not be tied down to these kinds of responsibilities.

My father was enraged. He said, "You don't have to worry about anything, your only duty is to obey us. I am your father not your enemy." So saying, he stalked out of the room. I wasn't going to give in to him. But my mother cried so much that it created a commotion. She had only one thing to say, "Get married, don't displease your father." Even then I didn't agree. So she went on a hunger strike. She is a heart patient, and so all my brothers and sisters forced me to say 'yes'.

What could I have done? I was trapped. But not even once did I reveal that I wanted to see my future wife. I knew that it wouldn't make any difference, and when my in-laws came to meet me, I locked myself in the bathroom, and did not came out until they had left. Those actions didn't make any difference. My mother, by now, had become very weak by starving herself, and I was forced to agree to their demand or else I would be responsible for her death.

They dragged me there on the wedding day and *nikah*, the marriage ceremony, was performed. That night I met that lucky (or unlucky) lady. She was sitting there all wrapped up and huddled as if I was going to attack her immediately. I wish I had the guts to tell her that I had no interest in the marriage, but she ought to have guessed that herself from my attitude. I removed her veil because I was feeling very irritated. At least I wanted to see her face. She was made up and *afshan,* the gold dust, was shining on her face and hair. She was a good-looking woman, and, if I had been interested in women, I would have been pleased. But as I have said before, I have an aversion to their gender. Anyway I said to her, "Don't be afraid, I am not even going to touch you. Tell me, where would you like to sleep, on the bed or on the sofa?" When she didn't say anything, I took a blanket and lay down on the sofa. Due to all the hustle and bustle of the wedding (and all the silly rituals) I was very tired and fell asleep right away. I woke up in the morning and I saw that my wife was lying curled like a bundle in the bed and sleeping. She had been crying and her kohl had smudged her face. God knows what she cried for! I didn't even touch her and hardly said two words to her. So I went into the bathroom, and when I came out refreshed, the breakfast was laid on the table and my wife and family were sitting there. They all looked depressed. I didn't say a word, had my breakfast, and went out. What else could I have done? My parents wanted me to get married, so I did!

After a couple of days my wife went to her parents' home and, as was customary, I had to go too. Every face there was downcast and it seemed as if there had been a death in the family, not a wedding. When my wife came back, I explained to her, "Listen, my good lady, I have only got married because of my parents' persistence. Otherwise I had no interest in this institution. Give me some time to come to terms with you, and you go back to your school, and your teaching to keep yourself busy, instead of weeping and wailing."

She understood what I meant and went back to her teaching. When my holidays were over I went back to America. I was bereft of any happiness. I didn't find any pleasure even in my friend's company. As soon as I finished my studies, I came back and got a job. But I felt awkward there. It looked as if my parents and relatives all had a question in their eyes, but they weren't asking me anything. During that period my wife became pregnant. Some idiots have a very romantic notion about having a baby, but who could explain to them that if there was any truth in it, no nation could claim to be more romantic than us, the people of the subcontinent.

Anyway, after nine months, in my mother's words a 'moon-faced' boy was born. My wife was very pleased as if she had found a toy to play with. To tell the truth I, too, felt that he was my son and I was responsible for him. I sent job applications both to America and to England.

Scientists were in demand so I got a job in England, and my son wasn't even a year old when all three of us came to England. My pay was enough for us to survive but we couldn't yet buy a house. So I asked my wife to send out job applications. She said that the baby wasn't even a year old so how could she leave him? I thought about it and said, "I will ask at work and seek other people's advice. The women in this country work; they send their children to the nursery or arrange for a childminder who looks after the children during the day. You should enquire about some arrangement like that or else we shall have to spend all our lives in rented accommodation." She started crying and said she would never leave her child with someone else. I hate weeping women. Women are naturally weak. There is no comparison with man's strength. Well, the man is the master, isn't he! Look at the lion, what strength, what splendour! Compared to him where does the lioness stand? Men and women have the same differences. I do not treat anyone cruelly but I can't stand stupidity, and sometimes I cannot control myself and I do lash out. But when she starts crying violently as if I had really abused her, then I cannot help but thrash her. People say that civilised and educated men do not raise their hand and beat their wives, but they haven't come into contact with women like my wife. Anyway, after weeping and wailing the next day, she started searching for someone to look after the baby. It was lucky that she found a job and a childminder on the same day, and she began life as a working woman.

After the day's work was finished she would come home with the baby and the shopping, then she would bathe the baby, put him to bed and then cook the dinner. Finishing the day's hard work I would have one or two pints of beer and when I went home, I would find her working. After the meal I would read the newspaper and then go to bed. My wife would do the washing-up and some ironing before her bed time. Next morning we would get up and go to our jobs.

If I get a cooked meal, clean and ironed shirts, and a clean house, then I demand nothing more. But I hate rudeness and idleness immensely. It is nothing to be proud of but it is a fact that whenever I have beaten my wife, I had done it on account of her peevishness or nagging. My son has grown up now and he realises that though I am a hard man, I am also fair. He has finished his education and is now working. He visits us sometimes to enquire about us. Our daughter doesn't live with us either. The children rarely speak to me, but they come to see their mother. I believe that they love their mother, but I have not come close to them. I don't know who is close to me? My wife? Certainly not. She is my life's partner. We have been living in this house for a long time, which is now ours. But the gulf which began between us when we started our life together has never been filled. My wife also works, she has always had a job. When she comes home she does the house work. She cooks the meal and waits for me. When I come back from work we have our dinner together, but we hardly say anything to each other. After the dinner I sit in the living room reading the newspaper or watching television. After doing the washing-up and cleaning the kitchen, my wife comes in and sits there and knits. Apart from the television or radio the only sound in the room is of her knitting needles. As if that is our conversation. I feel as if there never was a time to come any closer.

On that day she had knocked at my door several times informing me that the dinner was ready. When I went into the kitchen I saw that she had taken special care to lay the table. The table cover which was reserved for special occasions was spread and the special crockery too — the one which was bought for parties, although we hardly had any parties. I looked at her questioningly, but she was too busy serving the food. As we are not normally used to talking, I sat there eating quietly. She sat in front of me. When I looked at her face, I was stunned. I felt as if we had gone back twenty-five years in time. She was totally changed. There was make-up on her face, just like the wedding night when I had seen her for the first time. Her greying hair was jet black and she had *afshan*, the gold dust, on her forehead .

"What is that?" I asked her, surprised.

"What?" she too seemed surprised.

"What have you put on your face?" I repeated my question.

She touched her face with her hand, then showed it to me and said, "Nothing."

But how could I disbelieve my eyes. Her cheeks were red, and she had powder on her face and *afshan* on her forehead. But I kept quiet. After finishing the meal, she started to wash up. Her back was turned towards me and then I heard her saying, "This has been our last meal together." I said nothing, and she continued, "I am going to leave this house, forever and ever." Still I didn't say anything. As I have said before I hate silly talk. Then I heard her saying in a worried voice, "Oh, it's snowing, how they are going to come and fetch me?" And she started sobbing. I abhor weeping, and wondered why she had to cry if it was snowing. Again she said, "Do you know I am leaving home, I am leaving for good...?"

I thought she had gone mad. Why did she need to leave home, but I asked, "Where are you going?"

She said, "I don't know myself, they will take me there, but how will they come in this snow?"

I opened the windows and peered outside. It wasn't snowing but it was very dark. My wife remained sobbing, I wanted to say something to comfort her but I kept silent. The warmth of the kitchen was changing into freezing cold. She said, "I have decided everything, and I am ready. I will go outside and wait for them, so that they do not go away without me." She went out, and I wondered what had happened to her.

After a little while she opened the door and came in. She had her fur coat on, and was carrying her everyday shopping bag.

"Now I am ready." Then, pointing towards her bag she said, "All I have is here. I am returning your keys because I don't need them any more. I'll never come back to this house."

"Why?" I asked.

"This house is cold, it is quiet as a grave and dark." Surprised, I looked at her. She was wearing her wedding dress and she had tears in her eyes but *afshan* was shining on her hair and forehead.

Closing the kitchen door, she went outside. I heard the house door closing, then I heard a song. It was the voice of women singing. I opened the door and saw that they were coming towards my wife. It wasn't dark anymore. There was morning light everywhere. The women were carrying flowers in their hands. An old lady, dressed in a white silk sari with a red border, such as Bengali women wear on auspicious occasions, was leading them. The red *bindi* on her forehead was glittering. She took the shopping bag from my wife's hands and placed it on the lawn. Then she took her fur coat off and placed it beside the bag. I saw my wife was wearing her wedding dress. Then people started emerging from every side. They were of every nationality and race. And most of them were young people. I thought I should go and ask them who they were and where they were taking my wife.

I saw the old Greek builder who lived nearby. Quickly, I went to him and asked, "Where are all of you taking my wife?" He looked at me as if he didn't know me. Then he pointed towards my house and said; "She can't live in that cold and dark house. We have built a new house for her."

He walked quickly and mingled with others, and, singing something, they marched ahead. I remained standing there thinking, was it a hallucination?

(The title of the story in Urdu is *Sadaqat Husain Khan Ki Kahani, Un Ki Zabani.*)

HAMIDA MOIN RIZVI

WE ARE CIVILISED

Hamida Moin Rizvi *is from Sialkote, Pakistan. She obtained her Master's degree both in English literature and Urdu from Murrey College, Sialkote. When she came to London soon after her marriage, she took a course in Sociology, and got a postgraduate degree in Education from London University. Later, she did a diploma in TESOL. At present she is a lecturer in Chessington Community College. She runs an Urdu school which is partly funded by the Kingston Borough. She is involved in many cultural and social welfare projects for Asian women. Recently, Hamida was awarded a gold medal and a trophy for her performance by Murrey College on its centenary. She writes poetry and short stories. Two collections of her stories and one of poems have been published in Pakistan. She is also widely published in India. She lives in Surrey.*

I wonder why I have this terrible pain inside my heart — a very strange feeling which is making me miserable, almost killing me. I haven't committed a crime, have I? A murder perhaps. No, it is not possible. But why, then, is something haunting me? I keep looking at my hands — they look mutilated. I washed and washed them and they look the same. I have been shattered into pieces like a glass and I am unable to collect myself. It is so difficult — like collecting broken pieces of glass with my eyelashes — yes, eyelashes — ha! ha! poor eyelashes can't even hold my tears. It is a real mental torture, and will continue to exist until I remember something about myself, and the reason for this lingering sound. I sometimes hallucinate that my body has been turned into a liquid substance — weak and helpless, unable to do anything. At other times my inner-self turns into an empty dome, with harrowing darkness, and no doors or windows. There are demons of guilt screaming inside me. It is destroying my whole self. I feel as if I am walking on burning sands without shoes in a nightmare! I look in the mirror. I am no one. Who am I? "Oh God, please give me back my face," I pray. Give me back my identity. But when I recognised myself and I got my memory back I became sad and more miserable with unlimited regrets.

He sighed and looked outside the window of the train.

The red tulips outside remind me of something sinister. The footprints of my bleeding feet identify my existence. The smell of blood on my sticky clothes. The train going at full speed. I am running as fast as my legs can carry me. Someone is chasing me. I am running for my life. I am terrified. Then I hear a whistle of a passing train, the train stops or passes by — I am feeling dizzy and out of breath, and absolutely exhausted, when I see a door and enter it.

My head aches so much that I can't even open my eyes. When I force myself to look around I hear a blast; I faint, perhaps. The next time I open my eyes I cannot remember a thing, nor who I am. My whole body is paralysed. I have no control over any part of it. I try to scream but have no voice. Ages pass, it seems, when I feel a soft feminine hand touch my arms and say softly, "Don't worry, you are in hospital and quite safe. Don't move your hand, it has got a drip on. Keep your head still because you have a serious head injury and it is all bandaged."

With all his strength he tried to open his eyes. There was a big window to his right, and he could see the sky. He wished the window of his inner-self could also open and he could see inside.

A fresh breeze from his memory would enter to remind him of something. Anything that could make him remember happy times or even sad ones. The patient opposite his bed had fresh roses on his bedside table. *Oh, this is the season of roses and it is summer. The clouds in the sky do not mean anything. Why don't I feel any heat at all. Who am I?* He couldn't remember. *But why*? he thought.

"How are you?" The nurse spoke softly.

"What has happened to me?" he wanted to know.

"You injured your head, it needed many stitches."

"How? Where did it happen?" he asked, stunned.

"We don't know that. A drunken tramp saw you in the train at the station, he phoned the police and the police brought you here, the day before yesterday."

"But who am I?" he whispered to the nurse apologetically.

"Sorry, we have no idea. We couldn't find anything in your pocket to identify you. Your clothes were soaked in alcohol, but there was no alcohol in your stomach or in your blood. The police would also like to know whose blood was on your clothes apart from your own." *What does it mean, have I killed somebody*? He asked himself.

"Well, have some soup." The nurse helped him, but after the first spoon he didn't want any more. He put his head on the pillows and looked around the ward. There were only white people. *What area is this that there is not a single black patient in the whole ward. Indeed very surprising! Who hit me on the head, and why is someone else's blood on my clothes? I can't even think about having a fight with someone.*

"Nurse, what do you think? Who am I?"

"You look like an Asian to me, and your English accent is posh, that means that you were educated in a good school. It seems that you were brought up in the suburbs. I couldn't tell you any more."

"Well, one thing more, I don't feel that I eat meat," he said looking at the meat dish in the tray in front of him.

"All right, I won't give you any meat. Now take some rest." The nurse answered, picking up the tray. Then, like the other patients, he too lay down for an afternoon nap and slept. When he woke up, the nurse told him that two policemen had come to see him. Placing the tea cup on the trolley he wondered whether he had murdered someone? He began to feel a wave of nausea come over him — *Am I a criminal? No, no, never*!

"Good afternoon, Sir." Two police officers appeared. He gave them a blank look, and tried to move.

"Please don't get up. We just want to ask some routine questions. What is your name and address? How did you get hurt? Who were you fighting with? Did you hit someone?" Certainly there was only one answer to all these questions, "Officer, I don't remember anything."

"Your clothes were drenched in alcohol, can you remember anything about how it happened?"

"I just feel that I have never drunk alcohol, that's all." They looked at each other meaningfully, then got up to leave. "Well if you do remember anything, tell the nurse and she will call us."

Why aren't I worried if I am a criminal, and why wasn't I afraid of the police? The police were perhaps taking things easy, not really bothering to investigate further. He became curious, but any effort to remember drew a blank, and trying to remember made his mind tired.

So just to keep himself occupied he started to look around the ward. Visiting time had started and there was a stream of friends and relations. *Heaven knows if I have any relations. What is my age? How does my face look?* He hadn't even seen his face because of the bandage on his head. When the drip was taken off that evening, he went to the bathroom and, for the first time, saw half his face. Then, in the morning, when the bandages were off too, he saw his whole face many times. *This is my face, but it doesn't have any significance for me.* He was feeling as if there were many words and dots spread around him, but they were not making any sense. Nothing, that could provide him with any reference or connection to his life or identity, was there. He was tall and had a round face, brown complexion, big black eyes and black moustache. His age could be between twenty to twenty-five. After shaving, the face looked a little better. With unsteady feet he went to the ward, sat next to the bed and looked out of the window. His room was probably on the seventh or eighth floor, overlooking the street. The cobweb of roads stretched far, and a great many cars were running up and down the road trampling the earth, as if hurrying to some strange call. He was thinking, *If something happens to me, then I won't even know who I am! Is it important to know who has died? Colourful pretty birds are singing on the poplar tree. Why are they happy? "The infinite silence of this boundless earth makes me frightened." Yes, Pascal had said so. No, he was afraid of the unknown. How do I know about Pascal? Certainly it is not a revelation, I must have studied him. It means I am an educated person, but I...?*

"The doctors are coming to see you." With shaking feet he reached his bed and lay down. There were many doctors examining him and he kept on complaining, "Why aren't you doing anything for my memory? I will go mad. I don't even know where I can go after I am released from hospital." They told him that he was lucky to have been found and rushed to the hospital. He had been in intensive care for twenty-four hours. It would take time, and his memory loss was temporary. They went away. He sat in a chair and dozed. Again he dreamt the same scene — he was running, as if demons of terror were chasing him: the noise of the engine and the screams of the whistle. He woke up in terror, then slowly got up and went to the window. The evening meal was over and soon it would be visiting time again. Outside, the shadows of the trees had grown tall and the day was coming to an end. The orange rays of the sun were on his face.

A Concorde was flying away somewhere towards the South, and he could see a dome far away, a dome had some connection with his life, he felt. "Yes, it is a minaret of a mosque where people pray."

Yes, I will go there when I am better, perhaps I will remember something with this reference. The day is coming to an end, a nameless day. No, the day is not nameless, I am! According to the records at the foot of my bed, it is Wednesday today and the date is the twenty second of June. I can't find any clue to my identity just by knowing the date. The evening is slowly descending on the trees, houses and the grounds. He sighed and lay down in his bed.

"Hasn't anyone come to see you?" asked the patient next to him.

"I have lost my memory, and I don't even know if I have any relatives; if I do, then I don't remember them, and they don't know where I am or what has happened to me."

"Oh, that's no problem. Ask the police to show your picture on the television and your family will see it and they will know where to find you".

"That's a good idea! When they come I will ask." It was a good idea, but if he had murdered someone, then...!

The nurses were kind and other patients friendly towards him. The pain in his ribs was getting better, and he was getting stronger. But his heart was empty and time was passing. All he could do was to observe the dawn and the sun rising from the horizon. He would feel sorry for the withering buds in the hot sun and be irritated by the continuous chirruping of the birds. He would watch, from his window, the throng of people afflicted by a constant desire to rush to their destination. He had an excruciating headache all the time so he didn't bother reading the newspaper. He didn't have the strength to go to the television room either. He might have gone had he tried but he didn't feel like it. The hospital became quieter after nine in the evening, when the lights were switched off. But sleep was far away.

The police officers visited him again that evening, but he had the same feeling that they were not truly interested in any investigation. They had just come for a routine inquiry. They were neither interested in him, nor in solving his problem. They weren't bothered about the blood on his clothes though they did keep hinting, in a rather intimidating manner, that he might have attacked somebody. With a troubled mind, he got up and walked towards the corridor. On the duty nurse's suggestion he went to the common room. The television was on and a middle-aged man was sitting there, smoking. He was suddenly startled as if a bomb had hit him. *Cigarette, cigarette,* he repeated to himself, then ran to his ward. He developed a very bad headache and his condition was such that the nurses had to hold him to give him a sedative. The doctor made his rounds at ten in the morning and assured him that the ribs were healing and the wounds getting better. He told him there was nothing to worry about. When he was physically well, his memory would also return.

"Doctors never worry about anything, do they?" he said scornfully. The doctor gave an embarrassed smile and left. He was agitated. According to the doctors it had been more than a week since he had been admitted to hospital.

Sundays are usually very quiet in hospitals and the day passes even more slowly. The number of nurses and other staff was also less than usual. But there were more visitors on Sundays, which was painful for him. The nurse had told him that he could have his lunch in the common room. So he put on the funny dressing gown that the hospital had provided for him and went. After lunch, only those who wanted to have a smoke remained in the common room.

When he saw them smoking cigarettes he felt an intense disgust and loathing. He also had a strange kind of longing for one, which made him uncomfortable. He got up and switched on the television. The need to have a smoke was desperate though, mixed with feelings of fear and regret too. The *World at One* was on. The news was about an incident in a pub. There had been a National Front meeting when some Anti-Nazi League members arrived and a fight started. A member of the Anti-Nazi League died in this fight and one member of the National Front had been blinded. Then they showed the pub totally destroyed. About thirty or forty people were wounded. Some people had seen an Asian at the place of the incident, but the National Front denied that any Asian had ever been there. Because the majority of the witnesses supported the Front's denial it was accepted as the truth and the presence of an Asian was thought to be a mere fabrication by the Anti-Nazi League.

"Well, well! Fabrication... I, an Asian, went there. Joseph and I entered the pub together. He was the Australian who was killed. Joseph Morrell, my dearest friend. He was the son of an Australian businessman," he said to himself aloud.

"What did you say, that you went to the pub with Joseph?" A kind old man asked him.

"Yes, I did."

"Do you know your name?"

"Yes, my name is Asrar Mushhadi."

"Congratulations, your memory is back."

"Well, yes, oh! but Joseph... Joseph, oh! no." He held his head in his hands for a long time, then he looked up and softly asked the old man, "Where is this hospital?" Listening to the old man's reply he exclaimed, "What! Eighty miles from London! Oh...! May I ask you something?"

"Yes."

"Please don't tell anyone for the time being that my memory is back, I want to investigate something personally."

"I'm going home in the evening, so I won't blabber anything to anyone. If you need something, this is my address and phone number." He placed his hands affectionately on his shoulders and gave him his card, which Mushhadi took gratefully and sat there stunned.

It was Friday when Joseph and I had come to London to attend a conference against racism. Instead of going back the same day, we had decided that on Friday night and Saturday we would see London, and then go back to Glasgow on the night sleeper. We had had our meal at the Barbican, and then chatting and walking we had lost track of time and consequently lost our way too. The place was so quiet that we began to worry. We had to find a bus or the nearest tube station. Then there was one more problem when I realised that I had only one cigarette left and no matches. I had become so edgy needing a smoke that Joseph said, "Let's go back to the hostel and, with a bit of luck, some Patel's shop will be open and we'll be able to buy some matches."

"Yes, Patel's do open late at night," I answered. Joseph laughed.

"But it is nearly eleven now. Let's see, we might find a pub."

'The Kings Head' was glowing in red lights. So there was a pub nearby, well, well.

"Come on, problem solved," Joseph sounded relieved.

"Don't you start drinking," I warned, smiling.

"You know I am not a heavy drinker. I just want you to have your cigarette and matches so you'll stop worrying, that's all. That is friendship, isn't it? A friend in need — right?"

When we entered the pub some people stared at us. They had hate and anger in their eyes. Joseph had just stared back, but I was worried. I had never really faced rough and rowdy people like those present in that pub. Good manners and politeness make you a coward, there is no doubt about that. It was also true that Joseph could stand on a platform and deliver excellent speeches against racism, but he had not experienced physical encounters with racists. I pretended that I hadn't seen anything and went straight to the bar.

"A box of matches and a packet of cigarettes please."

"Hey you!" One man came near and growled. Then another. I looked left and right trying to act bold, as if I wasn't alarmed by the actions of these men. I asked the barman again, "A packet of cigarettes and matches please." Somebody shouted from the back.

"Didn't you know that blacks and dogs aren't allowed here?" someone else added.

"Then how come you are here?" Joseph stepped towards the group with great confidence.

"Don't you feel any shame when you talk like that? You, who are a citizen of a civilised country?" There was silence for a few moments, then a sneering voice, "It is you who should be ashamed of yourself. I know who you are. You spoke against racism yesterday and when I made a protest, the police threw me out. Don't you know that the white race is superior and it was created to rule? You're a traitor to your people."

Joseph spoke calmly, "You must be a spirit from the last century." Everybody laughed and the man stood up and roared. I put the money quickly on the counter and told the man that we just wanted the cigarettes and didn't want any trouble. He picked up both things and was about to give them to me when the shouts came.

"Don't sell any cigarettes to him!" He stopped.

"This is a civilised country. Such ignorance won't work here," someone standing up in the corner of the hall yelled, other voices rose in support.

"There are too many traitors here, while only nationalists are allowed here."

"Then you ought to have put a notice outside so that no one can make the mistake," I said very politely and held out my hands for the cigarettes. The barman also wanted to finish the arguments and extended the packet.

"Don't you dare!" The barman's hand stopped.

"All right, I'm going."

"You have insulted us, you can't just go like that," shouted a rough looking man.

"No, we are not going without our cigarettes and matches," Joseph said standing in the middle of a dozen or so tables, adding, "Don't worry, I'll report all of you."

"Never!" The man, who looked menacing, threw his glass aiming at Joseph's face, but Joseph ducked and some people started speaking up for us. Slowly I began to walk towards Joseph, so we could run to the door together. Now people had started fighting, and we only had a few people on our side—most were against us! They were making a circle around us. After swearing and shouting, they had started fighting. Glasses and

bottles were being thrown at us. Joseph staggered and I helped him, his blood was soaking my clothes and I tried to bring him out of the pub when suddenly someone yelled, "Don't let the black dog get out alive," and then a bottle was smashed on my head, and it became dark all around.

When I came to, I heard noises and banging and the lights were out. People were still fighting. How could anyone possibly know in that darkness whom they were fighting? There were noises of things being thrown and broken. I crept to one side by passing over some people, and there was a little dim light coming from somewhere outside and I could feel the cold breeze. I thought it was a door and I was right, probably it was the back door of the pub, because there were big drums lying around. My head felt so heavy as if the weight of one of those drums was on my head too. My head and clothes were soaked in blood, my coat was very sticky. I took it off and started to run, with the sound of fire engines and police cars coming from behind. I kept on running, alongside a railway line, and somewhere on the way my coat became entangled in a thorny bush and not having enough strength to free it, I left it there and just kept on running. My driving licence and my cheque book were in that coat, and may be my return ticket to Glasgow too. I entered a building — a railway station, probably. There was no one at the window of the booking office and nobody stopped me from going in without a ticket. I went straight to the first train standing at the platform, entered a compartment with great difficulty and just managed to sit down. It was then for the first time that I thought of Joseph. Why wasn't he here with me? The next moment it was dark again, I had fainted.

The Anti-Nazi people were asking the police to look for the body of that Asian who had come to buy the cigarette and matches, or find him alive. They insisted that it was very important that they look for him. The racists were saying that the Anti-Nazi League has made up the story, they had come to the pub just to create a disturbance, and the police thought so too. They did not believe that the Asian existed. Asians were too afraid to go to such a place at night, because it was a National Front area. The statement finished, so did the enquiry.

Very well, he thought, but he couldn't sleep all night and kept thinking. The first thing would be to ring his father and ask him to come here immediately. He would ask him to come at once by air. He is a barrister and it might be useful. Then he would reveal his identity to the police. The police were all in it as they were trying to hide and distort the truth. These efforts were being made by the National Front sympathisers who held key posts in the police. That's why even though he had insisted that his photo be shown on national television in order to discover his true identity, they would not agree to it. Maybe they knew who he really was and thought if his memory remained lost for over six months it would give them enough time to continue the case the way they wanted.

Oh Joseph, what have you done! I will never be able to wash your blood from my clothes, because you went to the pub for my cigarettes and matches.

I had met Joseph a year or so ago when we had both come for an interview in the same college. Joseph had soft, shining eyes: he always had a smile on his face, and his brown beard matched his long curly hair. He wore very simple and inexpensive clothes. Although he had attended the best schools, he believed in the equality of men whether it was economic or social. That's why he was an active member of the Anti-Nazi League. He would, with great enthusiasm, organise marches and arrange meetings. Wasn't he afraid of anything as we are? The fear of losing, fear which terrorises us with the frightening voices of profit and loss? What cowards we are! To compromise is cowardice in reality. I didn't plan this, I am alive but he is not! He was the one who stood there firmly for his ideals. He is the one who received the mortal wound and became immortal. Here I am, with a heavy burden of guilt on my head, and my feet are bloody travelling through life. My heart has turned into a ghostly tower where frightening silences prowl everywhere.

We talk about human rights, equality and freedom of speech, but in reality money has all the power! Because my father was a barrister and he knew our local area MP, I was spared by the police. Otherwise they would have arrested me for the murder of Joseph Morrell. That was the reason why they were neither serious about my case nor made any effort to solve the murder of Joseph. Our parents are not important enough to be able to break the circle of racist people who hold the key posts in the police force and in the civil service. That's why the murder of Joseph Morrell was being declared an accident, and no one was being arrested for it. Justice was not done! And I am left here to carry the pain and the burden of shame within me and suffer in silence as long as I live.

The train is running at a hundred miles an hour, and I hate the red tulips in the fields. They remind me of blood in my eyes. They are Joseph's blood. Now I am frightened of smoking.

This clean pure earth has a very murky and dusty sky; and its spiritual and physical world is wide apart. There is no consistency. There are different rules for different people... but they have just finished the task of civilising the whole world — isn't it wonderful!

(The title of the story in Urdu is *Ujli Zameen, Maila Aasman.*)

TALAT SALEEM

TIME AND PLACE

Talat Saleem *was born in Gujarat, Pakistan, but lived mostly in Quetta, from where she obtained her Bachelor's degree. Whilst still at school, her work was published in popular children's magazines. Since then her articles, poems and short stories have been widely published both in the UK and Pakistan. She is particularly known for her* Naat, *religious poetry, an anthology of which is currently under publication. She lives in Birmingham and teaches Urdu at South Birmingham College.*

Today Khurshid again brought home something that always created a crisis. It was a large packet of beef burgers. It happened all the time, at least often enough, that, when he came home from work, he would bring things like frozen pies, Kentucky fried chicken or steaks to eat. Nasima would explode, "What possessed you to buy this *Haram* food and bring it home?" Why should she cook it? She had decided that she was not going to fry anything today. She threw the packet on the table and, dejected, ran upstairs, sat down and started flicking through a magazine aimlessly.

Everybody said she had a mania, but what could she do? This belief had always been in her body and soul. She always had recognised the very clear boundary between what was *Halal*, and what was *Haram*; what was allowed by her faith and what was not. There was not any room to change that. It was not a mania, it was an ideology, a philosophy of life. Khurshid had called it a mania, a madness. All his friends and colleagues and their fashionable wives had changed so much. If not totally, then at least three-fourths of their personalities were now immersed in Western culture. There were no restriction in their homes as in hers. "Don't eat this, don't wear that or don't go there." In their homes there was peace and quiet and this freedom kept everyone happy. They lived in comparative comfort and ease.

Sometimes Khurshid was irritated, "These useless checks and controls have been unnecessarily imposed upon us," he would grumble. She listened to him talking to Wahid on the phone: "No, there is no way we can do that. This house belongs to Muslims, you know." It was a cutting remark clearly intended for her. "Life has become hell for me," he muttered, placing the receiver back. Throwing the magazine on the floor, she spoke from the steps, "Then turn it into a paradise and do what your dear friends do. To hell with me and my children. What are they going to learn from us, I wonder?"

"Will your religion allow us to do what we please?" He spoke emphasising the word 'religion'.

"Why is it only my religion, don't you have anything to do with it? No connections with you?"

Beef Burgers
Beef

"It doesn't matter if there is a connection, but I do not like the way you judge every thing by your religious yardstick."

"Then should I leave it for special occasions and do whatever you wish." Khurshid wanted freedom to enjoy life, but in a way that nobody would find out, like his friends were doing. They would eat what they desired, go where they wanted and their children would buy what they wanted. When Nasima went shopping she would read every packet for its ingredient. If there was something in them that Muslims were not supposed to eat, she would put the packet, even if it was her children's favourite, back on the shelf. Khurshid's friends would drink everything alcoholic or otherwise and visit pubs and clubs of all sorts. Their wives would accompany them. They were also Muslims, but his home was so different from theirs. Sometimes he would yearn for all that; at other times his blood would boil and he would start quarrelling. When his friends came to visit he would be ashamed for hours, as if Nasima had disgraced him somehow.

Ten whole years passed in such contention. There were no happy memories nor sweet moments from the past. Nasima's perception of her married life was confusing. "At times Khurshid behaves in such a way that it seems he does it just to annoy me." She thought she would not make any protests from now on. If he was not going to change, then she would change. Now she would keep herself in control, and he could do what he wanted and how he wanted. Whatever he said she would accept and stay calm. A few days would pass and then she would not be able to control herself and explode. Vehemently she would say, "Khurshid what has been happening to our life?"

"Nothing, my love, everything is all right," he would answer unconcerned and uninterested.

"Let me run the home for a few days as I would like to." She would try to charm him.

"Well, your religion is very strict, and you bring it into everything, unnecessarily. I am afraid to say a word, I know that instantly you will come up with your dos and dont's," he said mischievously.

"All right, I won't mention anything concerning food, dress and where we go and how we live."

"That's more like it. Everything has its place my dear."

"Then keep waiting for the moment when you can put the blame on me for being unreasonable," she would say angrily.

"No, no, please don't have a row now." He would make an effort to make her understand that for ten years their home had become a battle-ground, and only because of her religious fervour. "Let me run the house for ten weeks, and it will become heaven."

"To hell with a heaven where God's name is forbidden," she would snap.

"I am not against believing in religion, but I don't like it interfering with every little thing. I'm religious too, but everything has its time and place. And here you are imposing it all the time."

"What is the time to remember it, what time, what place?" She would become cross and turn her face from him. One day after such a crisis, somehow Khurshid made an agreement that in six months it would be her turn.

"You just watch quietly, and as God is my witness within six months our home will be the happiest home on earth. You just watch, my dear."

She was chained to this agreement. Indeed the home did become lively, but she was not happy with the way things were going, and deep inside her she was hurt. Khurshid was pleased and the children satisfied. The friends were delighted too. Only she was burning with an unknown fire within her.

"Well, your religion is on a holiday these days," he would smirk and laugh. "It will return to us but in six months time, till then it's a holiday," they would say in unison. She would become agitated, but, controlling herself, she would avoid an urge to retort. There were crystal glasses glittering on the shelf now for alcoholic drinks and the fridge was full of frozen non-kosher food. She could see it all and become distressed. Where would such freedom end? The thought that in the next six months she would take charge gave her comfort.

"In six months I will run the home the way I want to, won't I?" She would ask Khurshid, happy just thinking about it.

"Yes, yes, of course." *Oh God, please reward my patience! I'm living in this hope*, she would pray in her heart. *Please make them, please God, please, please*! There were only two months left before she would take charge of the house when the news of her father's illness came, and she rushed back home to see him. These months passed very quickly and when she returned, she realised that Khurshid had changed the decor of the house a great deal. For instance, there on the front wall of the room was a large size poster of a beautiful woman, scantily dressed, pouring wine from a goblet. The first thing she would do, she decided, was to take that down and throw it away. Khurshid seemed to be somewhat changed too. During the conversation he would stop, as if he were not able to concentrate. She was often surprised at his behaviour.

One evening, he surprised her even more when he wrapped his arms around her affectionately. Then taking her upstairs to the bedroom he said, "I want to say something to you. Please be patient and listen to me." For some unknown reason her whole body shivered.

"Before you went home I told you that I had to go to Turkey to see Sabir."

"Yes, you did. Have you been to see him then?"

"Yes, I have," he said swallowing, as if his throat has gone dry, "there I got married to his sister Ayesha."

"Got married," she was stunned and her face became pale. "What kind of a joke is this?"

"Joke! It's not a joke Nasima. Our religion allows us men to have four wives," he spoke emphatically. "I have not done anything wrong. We can have four wives—I can, my dear." Her eyes couldn't look at his solemn face any more. She bent her head quietly and was unable to say anything. What would she say? It was a straightforward matter. Khurshid had always told her, that religion had its time and its place, and this was the time, it seemed.

(The title of the story in Urdu is *Shesha-e-Dil Toot Gaya.*)

CHAND SHARMA

REPERCUSSIONS

***Chand Sharma** is from Chandigarh, India, where she obtained her Master's degree in Political Science. She is a writer and an actress. A collection of her short stories was published in 1995. Her works have been included in several anthologies of short stories and poetry. She set up Navrang Theatre in 1992, which produced her three feminist plays. She is a Labour Councillor for the Borough of Slough. The story included in this collection was written by her in English originally. She is presently writing a novel and her burning desire is to finish it, and to make films. Chand would have liked to earn her living by writing and broadcasting, but she pays her bills by working as a court interpreter in Gurmukhi, Hindi and Urdu.*

Mohan walked hesitantly into Seema Shukla's study and said, "Your telephone, Doctor Saheb." As usual she was buried knee-deep in her books and files. At this precise moment it was *The Prophet* which engaged her attention. Although she described herself as a staunch atheist, she considered this to be her Bible. The lines she was reading were, "Your children are your life's longing. They come through you but not from you, you can house their bodies but not souls."

She raised her head and looked at Mohan enquiringly.

"Who is it?"

"Some doctor's secretary, I don't know the name."

When Seema was not in the mood to talk to anybody or was busy in her work, Mohan always answered the phone and was not to disturb her unless it was really necessary.

"Is it important?"

"She says it is."

Seema was about to pick up the phone on her desk, when he asked, "Can I bring your tea now?"

"Yes, please—but if you are busy, I'll make it myself later." She attended to the phone as he left the room.

Seema was a very considerate employer. She treated Mohan more like a family member than a servant. She hated the way the middle classes in India treated their servants. Whenever she visited a fairly affluent friend of hers, she was appalled at their behaviour towards the servants. They did not get to taste the lavish meals prepared for their 'masters', but were expected to be at their beck and call every moment of the day or night. Late nights or early mornings, even at 3-4 a.m. when they returned from night clubs or parties, the old gateman had to stay awake to open the gate for them to drive in their cars.

Seema did not mind the house work, but she did not have the time. She often thought, if Mohan was not there to look after all these mundane jobs like cooking, cleaning, shopping, gardening and the rest, she would not have the time to do the important things in life like running her clinic in this rural area and day house visits. In her view, Mohan's contribution in allowing her to do what she had to as a doctor was invaluable.

"Dr. Shukla here," Seema said.

"I wanted to talk to Mrs. Sethi. I hope I've dialled the right number?"

"Ah! yes," Seema said, suddenly remembering the whole 'Mrs. Sethi' saga. Dr. Mathur would not see her, so she had invented that name.

"Any message for Mrs. Sethi?" She continued.

"No, I, I must speak to Mrs. Sethi personally ."

"I assure you, your message will be conveyed, she is my sister." Seema fabricated another untruth reluctantly.

"Dr. Mathur's strict instructions, I must speak to her myself."

"Well, she is not in right now, but you can tell me in confidence."

"No, I'm sorry." And the phone went dead. Seema stared at the receiver in amusement and rested it on the cradle.

"Dr. Mathur," she repeated that name to herself as if chewing it with distaste like a rancid dish to be spat out. She never liked eels and he seemed like a slippery eel, who wriggled out of situations, when he sniffed discomfort. She had made several efforts to see him but without any success. He was a successful doctor who worked in a society which suited him. Indians worshipped him like a god. They went to the temples every day, fasted on Tuesdays and Fridays, went on a pilgrimage. Nothing could fulfil their heart's desire, until it came to being blessed with a son. Only a doctor like Mathur was of any practical help.

His clinic was in a fashionable part of Delhi. A magnificent air-conditioned building with fitted carpets. The corridors of his clinic seemed like an art gallery with Renoirs, Monets and Constables everywhere. Just outside Dr. Mathur's room hung a reproduction of Van Gogh's *Sunflower* which suggested the blooming of the male children in their, as yet, barren garden of life. This luxurious environment screamed of his overwhelming success. Dr. Mathur's bank balance was not barren by any account. He had accumulated wealth by giving people what they wanted. They were not all wealthy people, but an obsessive desire to have sons had driven them from all walks of life to his door.

Some of them had saved for years to have enough money for the doctor's fee.

Once the sex of the foetus was determined, undesired results, i.e., female embryos were destroyed, without any hesitation. Even having indulged in such a practice for years had not diminished Dr. Mathur's enthusiasm.

He was the son of a wealthy, flamboyant businessman, Rajender Mathur, who had cared more for his luxuries than taking an active part in his son's upbringing. He was only two when his own mother died. While his father's new wife was nice to him initially, but once she had her own children, she could not stand the sight of him. The slightest thing would unleash her anger. Accidentally spilling his cup of milk, would lead to her tying him up and shutting him in the smallest room of the house without any food all day. Later, his father sent him to a boarding school and he never came home for holidays. His father could afford to pay for his summer excursions during the holidays. Rumour was that Dr. Mathur was a misogynist.

He had hired a London interior decorator to make the surroundings, where the doctor spent most of his life, pleasant. These material comforts possibly gave him an illusion of substituting the real comfort in his life. At the same time, the three-inch deep pile carpet cushioned the heels of those who trod over it, giving them an illusion that having a son in the family would cushion them from every jolt. When Seema visited his clinic in the guise of Mrs. Sethi, she was a bit surprised to see a Francis Bacon in one corner. She asked herself why he would want such a symbol of monstrosity around him. An epitome of ugliness incarnate, maybe it reminded Dr. Mathur of the ugliness that he was and she thought of her mother who had become a victim of such ugliness.

Seema was only four years old when her mother got pregnant for the second time. Seema felt rejected by her father, as he repeated often enough that he had wanted his first born to be a son. The image of her father's angry, contorted face was still fresh in her mind. That day he seemed exceptionally annoyed and shouted at her mother at the top of his voice, and, as usual, blamed her for not giving him a son. Seema could not be sure, but perhaps the baby was due any time and he was anxious just in case... it was another daughter.

Her mother stood at the top of the stairs. He stormed out of the room as she pleaded with him not to shout since she did not feel too well. Seema was at the bottom of the stairs looking at her mother and crying under her breath trying not to make any noise as he would beat her if he heard her voice. The next thing she saw... she shuddered at the memory, which still made her blood boil. He pushed her hard saying, "Go to hell, you bitch." She came tumbling down and landed at the bottom of the steps, hitting her head on the banister. As she lay there bleeding, he stepped over her and went out. Seema went running, called the neighbours, and an ambulance took her mother to the hospital, where she later died.

After her mother's death, her maternal uncle took her to his house where she was raised and educated to be a doctor. She never saw her father again and she never wanted to. Having no parents or other siblings, she often felt alone and dejected. To crown it all, her very dear friend, with whom she had shared many squabbles in the school playground, had committed suicide and Seema held herself responsible for it.

It was a fine spring day. As her clinic was not far from the rose garden, scented air wafted through it all day. Kadambini, like most of the girls at university, married as soon as she had finished her degree. As she came in, her usually smiling face looked deeply worried. She had two daughters and her husband did not make too much of a fuss, although he would gently let it slip — "It would be nice to have a boy." But her mother-in-law gave her an ultimatum — "If you don't produce a grandson for me this time, my son will divorce you and find someone else who can give him a son."

Kadambini's last words still echoed in her mind.

"Look Seema, it's a question of my life. I cannot afford to produce another daughter. I am five months gone, you know how this society functions, the way a divorced woman is treated. So what will I do? If it is a girl, I don't want her. What am I to do?"

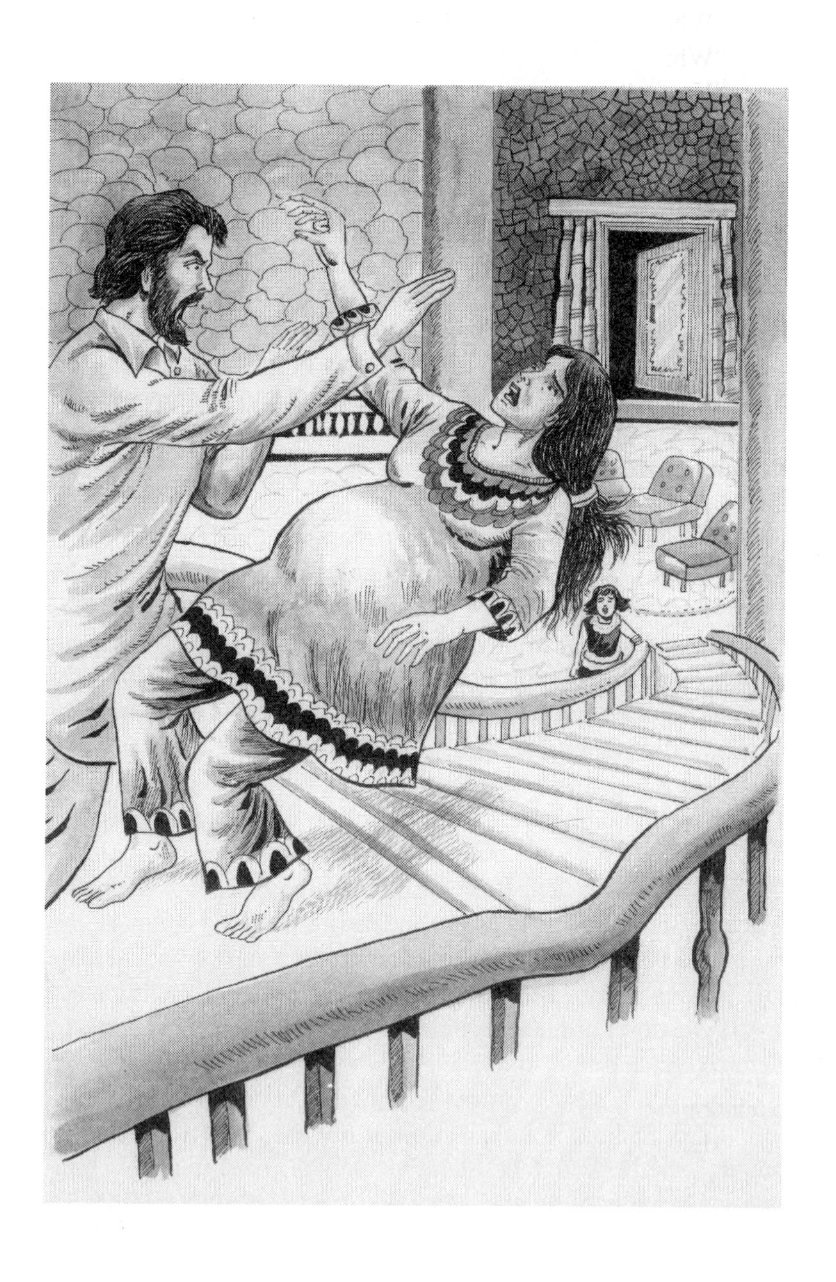

"Whatever an educated human being with dignity can do."

"What do you mean by that?"

"You are not some paralytic being. Be brave, fight injustice, that's what Lord Krishna says — To accept injustice is also a sin, not just to perpetrate it. I'm a doctor and my duty is to save life, not take it."

"Do you think it is right for them to treat me like an old shoe...to be thrown away?"

"No, I never subscribe to that view, in fact old shoes are more comfortable. Shoes have their uses, haven't they?" She tried to lighten the situation, "Without shoes one's feet can be injured by all sorts of stones, thorns, broken glass and all those sharp objects scattered in our path."

"That's not funny, Seema, I thought you were my friend."

"I am, but as long as women give in to blackmail and don't take a stand, nothing will change. Your dear mother-in-law... God! Aren't women, women's worst enemy?"

"Fine, I can go to Dr. Mathur."

She suddenly got up and left in a huff. A few weeks later Seema heard of Kadambini's suicide. It was then that she decided to take up the offer of a job with the World Health Organisation, although when she applied for it, she had not thought about it seriously.

After having spent over fifteen years abroad, in the Philippines, Africa, Latin America, etc. she was back home. She once again heard about Dr. Mathur. She wanted to confront him about his work, talk to him. But other than his patients, he would not see any woman. He never married, and was never seen with a woman. Disenchantment with women had begun with his hatred for his stepmother. He could not get rid of those bitter childhood memories associated with her. He seemed unable to form any relationship with a woman.

Hence one day, Seema pretended to be a certain 'Mrs. Sethi' to gain entry to his clinic. But it was a very brief and abrupt meeting. Having discovered that she was not a bonafide patient, he had asked her to leave as he was too busy to waste time while his precious patients waited. Seema did not reveal her real identity and left.

Since that encounter Seema had waited for an opportunity to see him somehow. She wanted to ask him a pertinent question, not in a letter, but to his face and she was keen to see his reaction, and hear his reasons for what he was doing. That occasion was provided when she received an invitation to attend an international conference on 'Embryo Research' being held in Delhi. She made inquiries and found out that Dr. Mathur would be there too. These days she lived in Nainital, a quiet district several hundred miles away from Delhi. She did not like travelling in discomfort. In India, the luxury of the motorway travel had not gone beyond wishful thinking as yet. After the Gandhi dynasty, there was no leader to steer the country onto a path where things moved forward. But one must do what one has to, come what may.

In the lavish lobby of Hotel Hyatt, delegates were gathering to check in. There was to be a welcome address that evening followed by a meal, so that delegates from abroad could meet and get to know each other. There were participants who had already met elsewhere and were delighted to see old faces.

After the meal, people sat chatting in the coffee lounge, split in groups. What Seema had often observed in foreign countries was true here too. Doctors and scientists from African nations, China, Middle East, and Europe were remarkably split in their respective groupings. Although there was a sprinkling of non-conformist gatherings as well, but few and far between.

She looked around, her eyes searching for Mathur's face. Although she had met him only once very briefly, she was sure she would recognise him. She had not spotted him earlier in the evening. Suddenly, in the far corner, she thought she saw him sitting alone. She had run into some doctors whom she had met during her stay abroad. Most of the delegates, having travelled long distances, had retired to their rooms, a few were still chatting and laughing.

She walked gracefully on the thick carpet with reassured steps. She loved black and often wore it. Today she was in a black sari, with a lovely turquoise border, and looked exceptionally good in it with matching jewellery. She did not wear jewellery often, but her sophisticated choice was becoming. Dr. Mathur sat there lost in his thoughts and took no notice of her as she got very near to where he sat.

While pulling a chair near him, she asked, "Would you mind if I joined you?"

"Why?...err...em...no."

"Thank you. Would you like some coffee?"

"No, it keeps me awake. Your face looks familiar."

His expression betrayed his thoughts. He looked at her face intently. Never before had a woman commanded his attention. It was the first time in his life he noticed anyone so closely. Her huge, almond-shaped, expressive brown eyes gave her a sombre philosophic look. He noticed how slim, tall and elegant she looked. He thought he never saw silkier hair than hers, spread like a shadow on her shoulders. He suppressed a strong urge to run his fingers through her long tresses. "With her slim and long fingers she could be an artist, couldn't she?" he asked himself. Her soft voice dragged him back to the conscious world, as she suggested.

"I could order some port or cognac for us?"

"No, not for me..." then suddenly he relented, "okay, whatever you like." He felt he wanted this moment to stretch. "Aren't you Mrs. Sethi?"

"No, I'm Dr. Shukla."

"Oh... maybe I'm mistaken. I'm sure... I thought you were someone else."

"Doesn't matter, everyone has a twin."

They sat there silently for a while, sipping their drinks. Seema wanted to ask him why he did what he did. She knew he felt uncomfortable in her presence, but she must get on with the business she had travelled here for.

"So how come you are here?" he asked her.

"Probably for the same reasons as you, but...maybe we apply our knowledge and training in different ways." Seema thought they were touching the edges of the territory she wanted this conversation to move on to.

"What do you mean?" Mathur did not seem to be in a mood for a heavy discussion.

"I wanted to use medicine to help those people who are deprived of the most basic needs like water or fuel. Hence I chose austere living for several years, working abroad in undeveloped countries. I know India needs me too and I am back here working in the villages. But you..."

"I...I did what?"

Seema did not want to sound or be rude to him though God knows he deserved it, she thought. But she realised that he felt terribly intimidated by her sudden presence and approach. Moreover she convinced herself that he was not very keen on her company... he may want to get up any minute and leave, as he had done in his clinic, several months ago.

"Do you hate women?"

Mathur got a bit unstuck, he was not prepared for such an abrupt and sudden direct attack. He would not have interpreted his work in that way. Seema continued, "When I was in London, there was a horrible incident...a man poured acid over several women in the tube...the underground train, and injured them badly."

"Yes, I read about it in the papers." He said meekly. She continued. "Then you also must have heard about another incident in Canada, where a man stormed into an office and gunned down many women. I can't understand such hatred for women. I thought that, maybe killing female foetuses could be another expression of the same desire."

Mathur had never compared his act of helping needy people wishing to have sons with such cruel acts. He had never indulged in the sort of introspection that Seema unwittingly pushed him into. *Is it how my hatred for my stepmother has manifested*? No...she is not there anymore. But he had no control on his subconscious, if that unconsciously ruled his conscious life.

"You are being unfair to me, I just provide a service which people need."

"But don't you think as doctors we have some responsibilities as well?"

"I do conduct my business in a responsible fashion."

"Just imagine, if female foetuses continued to be destroyed at this alarming rate, won't we reach a stage, when there will be no more females to produce males. Have you thought of the repercussions? A womb cannot exist outside a woman's body, not yet, anyway. Don't you think there will be an imbalance in society?" He looked at her incredulously, trying to hide a surging feeling of shock. His gaze followed her slim shadow as she got up silently and walked away from him. He could not look away until her figure disappeared from his vision.

(The story has the same title in Urdu, and was translated into English by the author.)

SAFIA SIDDIQI

COMMUNITY LEADER

Safia Siddiqi *came to London from Rawalpindi. She wrote poetry and short stories, but later she concentrated only on short stories. Her short stories have been published in India and Pakistan and her articles have appeared in Urdu papers of the UK. She writes a column for* Ravi, *a weekly published from Bradford. Two collections of her short stories have come out, as well as an Urdu translation of Marion Molteno's book,* A Language in Common. *The third collection of her short stories is soon to be published. She lives in London.*

Adjusting his tie for the fourth time, Mr. Chaudhry looked around him. The guests had started arriving. He looked carefully at his own suit. It was such a change from the misshapen trousers he had worn continuously for the last one year, off and on, that is. It made him feel conspicuous, as if all eyes were on him. It made him feel uncomfortable. Still, he kept himself under control, except for a nervous twitch of the eyes, and a shaking of the hands. He smoothed his jacket, removed the imaginary particles of dust from his sleeves and wondered how he was going to make up the money he had spent on his clothes. He couldn't really afford them. The suit was not such a problem: five pounds a week off the housekeeping and in twenty weeks the suit would be his. But the shirt, the tie and the shoes were also expensive. For a moment he became worried and stood thinking, "Oh! my God, all this adds up to a lot," and was lost in thought for a while. Slowly, worry was replaced with satisfaction as he pondered over the long term prospects. "On the other hand," he thought, "it is not as bad as it seems. It is an investment. It may not earn me money, but I can earn respect and status, and then my family will certainly be proud of me." He felt reassured and a smile appeared on his face. It was at this moment of relief that there was a tap on his shoulder. He looked around to see Miss Simpson looking at him.

"Mr. Chaudhry," she enquired, "how are you?" With Miss Simpson's arrival he was sure that his *Eid* party was going very well, although there weren't many Pakistanis present. After guiding the guest to the table he remembered that they already knew about our customs and traditions. It was more the English neighbours and friends who needed to know about those things. Pakistanis knew about *Eid*, and they celebrated it themselves.

"If we are going to have an *Eid* party, we ought to invite those people who don't know anything about our religion, and need to be introduced to the good points of our culture and traditions." He felt very proud as he remembered the scene where he had delivered those words to the newly-formed committee. They were impressed and requested him to accept the important task of drawing up the guest list.

He had made the list very carefully and included the members (or officers) of the local authority, the MP for that area, social workers, community workers, Community Relations officers, and the local news reporter. And it was just a coincidence that most of them were women. Mr. Chaudhry had gone around with the invitations and made a personal request also. It was the first function to be held by the Pakistanis of that area and most people saw it as a useful opportunity to meet leaders of the Pakistani community, to learn about them and to understand their problems. Only the editor and the MP had sent their regrets.

Mr. Chaudhry looked around him. The guests seemed to be enjoying the samosas and sweets. Mr. Chaudhry, being the chairman of the society, had received them, said a few words of welcome and gratitude. He had made sure that those who could be useful would be given the warmest welcome. Suddenly, in the crowd, a beautiful redhead floated into view and he knew instantly that it belonged to Miss Wood. She was looking around hesitantly, her blue eyes apprehensive. Perhaps she didn't know anyone in the crowd, and couldn't decide where to go. Mr. Chaudhry saw his chance and strode towards her, held her by the elbow and moved towards the table. And, with the same deftness that he used to serve his customers, placed a teacup in her hand and a plate full of refreshments on the table. He liked Victoria Wood very much. She worked in the Community Relations office and, whenever he had any problem, he would go to her.

It would not be an exaggeration to say that he would look for any excuse to visit her. If he himself did not have a problem then he would offer to help a friend or neighbour. He felt very pleased as he thought that she would certainly be impressed today, and she looked so beautiful. Mr. Chaudhry, as usual, looked at her closely; her curly unmanageable hair was carefully done and tied with a pink ribbon. She wore a pink blouse of the latest fashion which had buttons at the back, as if it had been worn the wrong way around by mistake, the low cut revealing her soft, white back. Whenever Miss Wood would sweetly call him 'Mr. Shawdry,' his heart would melt. He wanted so much to call her Vicky, like others in her office, but did not dare. However, he was beginning to feel hopeful now that he was becoming a Community leader, and might call her not only 'Vicky', but also 'my dear Vicky' and 'my dearest Vicky'. Within a year or two his dream would be fulfilled. And today, amongst his respected guests, attired in his new suit, shaking hands and exchanging pleasantries, he felt very confident that his plan would be successful. He refocused his gaze taking up the totality of her figure, cutting through the layers of clothes like scissors to reveal their hidden secrets. He liked what he saw. Suddenly he was awakened from his reverie.

"Mr. Chaudhry, nice party," Miss Verma addressed him.

"Thank you, Sheila," Mr. Chaudhry smiled confidently.

"Mr. Chaudhry," she moved closer, "are you old-fashioned? I mean you don't really approve of women mixing with men, do you?"

"Pa... r.. don?" Mr Chaudhry tried to divert his attention from Miss Wood and tried to concentrate on what Miss Verma was saying. She continued, "What I mean to say is that there are no Pakistani ladies present in this party. Do you keep your wife in 'purdah' Mr. Chaudhry? Does your religion forbid the meeting of opposite sexes?" Mr. Chaudhry felt irritated by her questions. Just because she is an Indian she likes to put us Pakistanis down. But he could not ignore her as she, too, was a Community worker. He patted Miss Verma on the shoulder, and with an indulgent smile said to her, "This is not the time or place to talk about religion, my dear — oh! your plate is empty." He quickly brought a tray of sweets to her and then, making sure that none of his friends could overhear, said in a condescending tone, "I can't say about the others, but I never do anything, or make any decision without consulting my wife. My youngest child wasn't feeling well otherwise my wife would have been here." He made a mental calculation to remember how old his youngest child was, in case Miss Verma fired more questions about his family. After satisfying Miss Verma, he looked again towards Miss Wood, who was speaking to a young Englishman. He felt a pang of jealousy. Suddenly a tall girl materialised before him.

"Are you Mr. Shawdry?"

"Ye... e... s?" He was startled as he did not know this girl, who looked quite aggressive and intimidating.

"I'm the correspondent of the local newspaper. Could I ask you a few questions?" And then she started firing questions at him with such rapidity that he could not understand a word. This party was the first of its kind, and its hectic pace had already taxed his mental capacity to the limit and he was exhausted. He understood only a few words of her questions, which were familiar to his ears such as 'ethnic minority', 'racial attacks', 'integration'. 'exploitation' and 'physical abuse'. He had heard them before on TV and radio but their meanings were not clear to him and he could only make guesses. For a moment he was lost for words. *How am I going to get rid of this woman!* Whenever the girl stopped to start a new sentence, he nodded as if he had understood her completely, and would sometimes say, "yes", or "you are right", or "I hope so". His knowledge of English, which he had learnt at work, had its limits. His chance came when she stopped at the end of a sentence and he grabbed a plate from the nearest table, loaded it with some samosas and sweets, and held it to her, "Have some samosas, they are delicious," he said and quickly proceeded in another direction. She had made him very self-conscious and nervous. He kept looking over his shoulder, and when he saw that she was speaking to Mr. Hussain, he breathed a sigh of relief. Mr. Hussain was the General Secretary of the society and he could easily provide all the answers in English.

The party was proving a great success. Afterwards Mr. Chaudhry, along with a few friends, went to the nearest pub to celebrate. During the conversation someone mentioned his child not being well, then he too, suddenly remembered that one of his three children had not been well for a few days. Which one he couldn't exactly remember. Then he remembered what his wife had said when he had been getting ready for this party. She had asked him to telephone for the doctor. "Bloody woman," he felt furious, "she can't do a damn thing herself," and had left without doing so. Even the thought of his wife and children made him depressed and weary. He extracted some coins from his pocket, placed it on the counter and left. Now that he was enjoying himself, he felt good and pleased with himself. To hell with the wife and children. Would they never leave him alone?

Driving towards home, he kept thinking of the party and its success—the people who had come had expressed their thanks and appreciated the need for such gatherings in future. Members of his Executive Committee had also been effusive in praising him for the success of the party. The photographer from the Asian newspaper had been there, and soon photos would appear in Asian newspapers and magazines. The people of his community would be impressed. Sitting in his car, he felt very important and his chest swelled with pride. His planning was perfect, he told himself over and over again, and a wide grin stayed on his face all the way home.

Mr. Chaudhry's preoccupation with social advancement in the community was only two years old. He was happy packing curry powder and selling cornflakes, until he saw a photograph and the accompanying article in an Asian newspaper. The photograph was of one of his old friends. Both had arrived in England together from Pakistan to seek their fortune. They had lived and worked in London together before their paths divided, and his friend moved to Birmingham. He often wondered about his whereabouts and amused himself thinking of his friend's surprise were he to see him now. How prosperous he had become! He had his own house, a car and owned a grocery store. If he hadn't read the article he would never have recognised his old friend. The photo had been taken at the inauguration of an imposing new warehouse which was being opened by the local MP. The article first surprised him, then made him feel very frustrated. His friend had started by buying a small factory in Birmingham which got bigger and bigger. He had a thriving business now, owned one of the largest factories and many shops and was a very rich man as well as a respected member of his community. The article disturbed Mr. Chaudhry, and slowly destroyed every bit of the confidence he had gained. He found that he couldn't sleep for many nights.

He used to be proud of himself, whereas now he only felt small, working in his little grocery store, and kept thinking that he hadn't really achieved anything in spite of hard work. He would say to himself that working in the shop had improved his English and he could now frankly say "yes dear", "no dear" without feeling shy, and he could easily swear in English when young troublemakers came into his shop. He gave the matter a great deal of thought and then the first thing he did was to change the name of his shop. 'Chaudhry Grocery Store' became the 'Chaudhry Self-service Store' and a few changes were made around the store as well. He started reading Asian newspapers and magazines regularly. He would read about different organisations in cities, the functions being held and the photos published. Now and then there would be statements from different community leaders about their meetings with MPs and other important people. Sometimes people wrote letters, appreciating the work of their community leaders. He began to feel the urge to help his community, and though it would be hard work, he thought the rewards would make it worthwhile. He believed it made one famous in the community and that fame brought respect and recognition. The Society was formed and gradually the desire for importance engulfed his entire being. Every step of his began to be motivated with this thought. Now he appeared very friendly and kind-hearted. There was nothing he wouldn't do for his people. Lots of things required his attention: someone's sick child needed to be admitted into hospital, a dead body of someone's relative had to be sent back home for burial, a husband, whose wife was waiting in Pakistan for her visa. He would offer advice and support and work tirelessly for his community after locking up the shop. He was the chairman of the society he had formed with the help of his friends and it made him feel important. He carried a heavy burden of responsibility. Sitting as the Society's chairman, he would feel that his personality had changed tremendously. He felt elevated. His responsibilities grew and so did his popularity. The simple people of his community sought his advice and help in every matter as he was a man of importance. He would gladly comply, no matter how busy he was. He enjoyed visiting Community Relations offices and he would go to great lengths to find an excuse to meet Miss Wood. When she spoke to him her voice would ring like music in his ears, his eyes would light up like two burning candles at the feet of the Madonna.

He kept the photograph of his friend, and now and then, he would look at it as if to keep his determination undiminished, and his dreams alive. One thing though, kept nagging him like a thorn in his flesh — it was his friend's fashionable wife, highly visible in the photograph, standing beside her husband. This made him find his own wife even more repulsive. He had been betrothed to his cousin at a very early age when he had been indifferent and ignorant of the importance of marriage vows and had never given the matter any consideration. When he came to England, there were only two things which dominated his mind — earning money and enjoying himself. He liked those girls who made themselves up with beautifully painted nails and fancy hair-dos. They would gladly go out with him even though he wasn't their sort. He loved having a good time and had never thought of getting married and settling down. Life was too good to think of anything seriously. And then he went home to Pakistan to meet his parents, and, within a few hours of his arrival, he was reminded of his obligation to take the wife who was waiting for him. He was the knight in shining armour for someone whose face he couldn't even remember, and wasn't ready to love. He simply refused to marry her but, when he was told of the disgrace his refusal would bring upon his entire family, and the fact that the girl's parents were dead, meaning that she was their (or rather his) responsibility, he weakened and had to yield. He was his parents' only child and was obliged to fulfil their wishes. He could never let them down. But he made up his mind never to give this girl the true status of a wife. She would remain in that country, he thought, determinedly, and he would never send for her. But fate had something else in store for him. His father died a year after his visit and his mother was left all alone. When he wrote and asked her to come and live with him here in England, she flatly refused.

How could she go and live with him and leave her daughter-in-law alone in Pakistan? Partly out of love for his mother, and partly to avoid the ridicule of his community for abandoning his mother, he sent two one-way tickets, and his mother duly arrived with her daughter-in-law. Mr. Chaudhry had no emotional attachment to his wife, in fact he never gave her any thought. It was as if he had decided not to like her even when she eventually became the mother of his child. He put up with that young girl only for the sake of his aged mother. He still nurtured the hope that one day he would marry the girl of his dreams and his mother would not be there to blackmail him with the talk of family honour.

He detested his wife for spoiling his chances to have a modern wife whom he could show off to his friends and important acquaintances. Things did not turn out as he had hoped — they never do. When he returned from the airport after sending his mother's coffin back home he realised that things would remain the same. He was not young enough to start a new life with a new woman, and also not wealthy enough to afford three children and two households. Life went on as usual; him finding faults with everything his wife did, she suffering in silence. Since Mr. Chaudhry had assumed the responsibilities of serving his community, he became so involved that often he didn't even see his children for days. Gradually, he became so detached that he had to think hard to remember their faces. He had been extremely busy in the preparations for the party, and he kept thinking that things could have been so much easier had his wife been able to share some of his social burden.

He reached home and the car came to a stop, and with it his train of thoughts. "It has been a nice day and a successful party," he said to himself. Then he opened the car door, got out and entered the house. As soon as he came in, his wife came down and followed him to his room. It irritated him.

"What is it?" He growled.

"Please ring the doctor. The little one is very ill. He has very high temperature and hasn't had any milk since morning," she was crying. He got angry at this invasion of his happy mood and snapped at her.

"Woman, you can't even call the doctor when you need to," he threw his jacket on the chair and picked up the phone. She went upstairs wiping her tears, her steps unsteady. Mr. Chaudhry had just opened the door for the doctor when there was a thud upstairs, and the children started crying.

"Am I too late?" the doctor was startled.

"No, no it is only the children crying."

When he and the doctor reached upstairs, his wife was lying on the floor, and the two older children were clinging to her crying loudly.

"Oh my God!" the doctor ran towards her, and felt her pulse. "Nothing to worry about, she has just fainted, she seems very weak." After examining the mother, he checked the sick child and said to Mr. Chaudhry, "I think it is best that both of them be admitted to hospital, so that they can be properly looked after. I'll phone for the ambulance." Mr. Chaudhry wanted to tell the doctor that there was no need to send his wife to hospital, but things happened so quickly that he was unable to say or do anything.

When Mr. Chaudhry received the call from the hospital to go and see the doctor, concerning his wife's medical report, he was in a foul mood. He had so many things to do; there was the shop, and the society's meeting, and he had been blessed with an opportunity to go to the Community Relations office. He cursed his wife from the bottom of his heart. When he arrived at the hospital, he told the doctor of the many important tasks that he had to do, and the doctor apologised for asking him to come and requested him to be seated.

"Mr. Chaudhry," the doctor began, "I'm really sorry to inconvenience you, but the situation is serious, and I had to see you." He held some papers in his hands, "We have just received your wife's report; X-rays and tests we did, I'm very sorry to say that your wife has TB." He stopped for a moment. " It seems that it is on the second stage, but there is no need for alarm, as we now have means to treat it. Modern medicines are quite effective." He shuffled some papers on the table, held one piece of paper, read it carefully, placed it in the front, "But Mr. Chaudhry, one thing is very important. She has to take a positive attitude and take extra care of herself, which includes being happy." Mr. Chaudhry felt like throttling the doctor for these suggestions.

In the women's ward of the hospital, the staff nurse was busy trying to solve the mystery of bruises on the wife's body , with the help of an interpreter. She was asking her how she came to receive them, and the wife, instead of replying, swayed her head from left to right and kept saying no, no. This had been her best kept secret. She couldn't tarnish the reputation of a Community Leader by such a vile accusation as wife-beating. Could she?

(The story has the same title in Urdu.)

NAJMA USMAN

CLASSIFICATION

Najma Usman *is from Pakistan. She did her MSc in Organic Chemistry from the University of Karachi. After coming to UK she worked for a while in industry, and the she joined PRA in their research projects. She is presently teaching languages in Thames College for Adult Education. She writes poetry and has recently started writing short stories as well. Her poems and stories have appeared in many Urdu magazines of the UK and Pakistan. An anthology of her poetry has been published earlier and a second collection of her poems has just come out. She lives in Surrey.*

"It is decision-making day today, the biggest decision of our lives!" Standing on the north side of the garden, she pondered. The peonies were blooming for the first time this year; red flowers with rose-like petals, swinging at the end of the branches, their weight making the plants bend to one side. The fence was quite tall on this side, and the next door neighbour's apple tree branches had given shade to the plants near it. Propping her knees on the knee-pad, she thought it was nice that the peonies got the shade of the apple tree, otherwise the sun would have scorched them, had they been planted on the other side. Plants and trees too need suitable surroundings to grow and bloom — just like us humans. She started to clear the weeds around the peonies. The weeds were growing in abundance and some had yellow flowers. How quickly they grew and spread everywhere, she thought, and how fast was their cross pollination. You pulled them out, and just a few days later they would grow back again. The things we look after and care for, get damaged so easily, whereas useless and painful things, like weeds, are always in abundance. Whenever she saw the weeds around the plants, she always thought about that. It would be really nice to have only those plants, flowers, and trees which we liked and wanted, and for which we planted seeds, watered and tended them. The sun was going down and the heat becoming bearable. It even felt a bit chilly.

She gathered all the weeds she had cleared and, placing them in a black bag, she took her gloves off. She looked at the peonies fondly. The plants were clear of weeds now, and standing on their own, looked quite confident, the flowers even prettier now that they had some space — breathing space! Yes, I think that is the word I was looking for, 'breathing space'. Perhaps these blooming flowers would not feel suffocated now. 'Suffocation', but what could she do to get rid of the things that were suffocating *her*? What weeds in her life could she pull out and throw away, and how? Whenever she tried to get rid of this choking feeling and clear the atmosphere she felt even more smothered. Whenever she tried to pull out the weeds from her life, it made her hands bloody

and also bruised her heart. Relationships were even more damaged, and emotions exhausted. She was tired and weary of this life which treated her so badly. She felt that even her soul was battered, and now she had reached the end of her tether. She could not go any further. Enough was enough, she could not live a life of pretence; living as others wanted her to live and not how she perceived the world. She could not put up with what other people said, "Don't bare your soul to your parents because they are old and frail and cannot face the disgrace. Don't let the children see that you are unhappy and miserable, that will disturb them and it might affect their future." Decisions, decisions — making decisions kills you sometimes!

Decisions are strange things, and some of them turn your life upside down. The decision to get married, the choice of a partner with whom she was going to spend her life, had been made very quickly. Her mother had shown such haste to marry her off, even though Farah had only just finished her BSc exams. Her father could have thought about it, but why hadn't he? He was an educated man, and a successful businessman too. But the truth of the matter was that, having been to England and possessing a British passport, had concealed her husband's weaknesses and shortcomings. He had, quite easily, become qualified to be a suitable match for her. I wish father had known and tried to understand the philosophy of science.

In the classification of elements there is a principle that if two opposed substances are put together, they often become poison for each other.

She took a deep breath in the cool, clear air. How calm and quiet the garden was, and how beautiful it looked now; clean and full of flowers. She collected the shovel and gloves and came to the kitchen. It might rain today. This was typical London weather for you. Sometimes spring would arrive in the middle of March; and sometimes the rainy season would continue till May, even June. She put the kettle on as it was almost four o'clock, and her husband would be back from work by half past five. Then he would take the remote control in his hand, collapse on the sofa, and start changing the channels. In the beginning she had found this habit quite amusing; now we are watching wrestling, now pop music, now a dramatic scene, next minute, golf. But then it began to irritate her and she would say, "What are you doing? Why don't you watch something instead of changing it all the time?" He always ignored her. How different they were. Amir was impetuous and rash, quick to make decisions and regret them later. And Farah, calm and serene, like a slow-flowing river!

They were so different in every way. She liked to watch drama while he preferred American movies. She enjoyed savoury, spicy snacks with her tea, and his evening would start with a glass of whisky. Farah liked to sit in the dim light, and he wanted all the lights on.

"I don't like the shaded lights in the room," he would snap. It wasn't that Farah didn't try to compromise. She did her best. She even started to watch American films and got used to sitting in the blazing light, but she didn't come to terms with his habits and hated the smell of whisky. When he started his drinking, she would leave the room. They lived under one roof but they were like strangers to each other. They were so different that, in the hope of trying to understand each other, they made things even more confusing. The negative emotions and hostile attitude had continued to grow all through the years and they had drifted so far apart that even if they tried, they couldn't come close. Now they had arrived at that stage when, if any positive emotion dared to surface, it would die instantly. If you planted a weeping willow next to a cactus, would it bloom — certainly not!

When the children were young, there had been occasions that warranted their mutual participation, and both of them had contributed happily and sincerely. Admission to school, term reports, parents' evenings, choosing the colleges and higher education, these were their shared happy times. But their lives followed two different paths. The blessing of a busy life in London is that you don't meet anyone unexpectedly. Most of the time you meet friends at weekends, or at parties; nobody comes to see you without an appointment. Within the four walls of the house, when they didn't have to pretend, their real feelings and the naked truth of drifting apart would often appear so suddenly that it was not possible to ignore them. During that period the question of separation entered their minds many times, but the children and their future always stopped them from taking the final step. When the children were young, they needed both parents; when they were growing up, any kind of tension would have been upsetting for them. After that, the question of their marriage took precedence. They were fortunate that this matter was resolved happily and quickly. Their daughter married a doctor and went to live in Dubai. The son got married and went to America with his wife. While making the tea she was thinking that this would be the first summer they would spend without their children. Who knows how many seasons they would have to endure, both of them together, but really alone! She came into the sitting room carrying her tea, and suddenly felt exhausted. She felt that these days she got tired very easily. Perhaps it was her age, she wondered. Amir, too, was going to retire in a few years' time. Farah always had part-time jobs, but now she felt she couldn't even do that. She felt this constant tiredness. Perhaps it was the monotony of her life that was making her feel like that. How would they continue their life's journey? That was what they were going to decide today. Whenever this question had arisen earlier, they had both decided, not yet! Not while the children were living at home. Now that the children were secure in their own lives, the parents wanted to get out of this rut and be free and happy.

She felt very depressed. How strange that they had spent such a long period of their life rejecting each other. Though they had tried to make some compromises they were not enough. They also had changed with time, she realised. She still relished savoury snacks at tea time, but now she had so many stomach ailments that she had to be very careful and avoid those snacks. Amir still liked his drink but doctors had warned him that his excessive drinking might damage his liver even more. Things on the outside had changed but within themselves they had not. She often thought that she was a misfit for Amir; perhaps she was like a desert flower which was planted in a spot where it always rained, and this continuous rain had made its roots rot. Sometimes the dry season came and stayed for a while and the plant would begin to take root, and a new shoot of hope would show its head, but just then the rain would start and so would the decay — and this process had continued for many, many years.

The clock showed half past five and he was back, but he looked tired and weary. He got hold of the remote control as usual and dropped down on the sofa.

"Listen, if you want to talk, I'll make some tea. You know I don't like the smell of whisky," Farah commented standing at the kitchen door. Amir was looking at her with a blank expression on his face.

"I don't want any drink today, I feel very tired." He wasn't even changing the channels as he always did. She brought her own cup of tea into the room, and for a long time they both sat quietly together. At last Amir spoke, "One of my friends has come back from America; over there he met our son, who is very happy and settled and has a good job. Now, our son wants to invite us both to live in America." He stopped, then spoke haltingly; "Will you come... won't you... to our son?" Farah was looking out of the window. The honeysuckle had spread over the fence, and there was that wild climber clinging to its thin branches. She had pulled out the wild climber many times but it grew back and clung to the branches of the honeysuckle. There are exceptions to every principle of science, she thought. Perhaps the honeysuckle and this climber are parasites living on each other. Perhaps they cannot survive alone.

(The story has the same title in Urdu.)

NAEEMA ZIAUDDIN

PRECEDENCE

Naeema Ziauddin *is from Sargodha, Pakistan, where she was educated. After her marriage, she came to live in Karachi where she did translation work for magazines. She is a prolific writer and her writings are published extensively in India, Pakistan and England. She writes short stories, poetry, travelogue, and articles on literary, political and social topics. The first collection of her short stories has just come out. An anthology and a travelogue are soon to be published. She lives in Germany.*

Herr Oliver Strein was extremely worried. Everywhere he went he carried this worry with him. When he went to the garage and picked up a shovel or fork and tended the flower beds, or when he mended the fence, we could see that he was terribly upset. Even when he started his car engine and tinkered with it, the sighing and deep breathing could be heard. Whenever I went in to the garden, to hang my washing and in the evening, to collect it, or when I meant to tidy the garden and sweep the fallen leaves, I could hear Herr Oliver Strein's 'ohing and ahing', and his heavy breathing would be like an assault on my ears.

"Poor Herr Oliver Strein is very worried," informed my husband. Agitated, he would come in, then go out and try to comfort Herr Strein. He would recount some old jokes to him, relate some racy anecdotes which are typical of men's gatherings. He would talk of recent happenings or the weather, anything that could make Herr Oliver Strein forget his worries and also, those beer cans, which were in his hand all the time. He was terribly depressed and disturbed, so it continued like that for some time. "Could you get lunch a little early?" my husband asked just before noon.

"What do you mean, early?" Surprised, I looked at the clock and then at him.

"I have to go with Herr Strein."

"You have to go, where?"

"To take Oto to the vet."

"Oh yes, I had forgotten. How is he now?"

"Same as before," my husband sighed, "there is no change in his condition. Herr Strein is very worried now."

"Yes, I have been listening to him."

"Listening, what do you mean?"

"Oh! I mean I have seen him. Poor thing, how he breathes loudly, and sighs..."

"All right, all right."

All three of us sat in the car with Oto and the entire evening was spent at the vet's. The vet decided to keep Oto and we came back. Next day, Herr Oliver Strein was even more worried. His face was a true picture of his distress, as was evident from his every move, and from his sharp and loud breathing which followed him everywhere like a shadow. His beer-drinking habit had made his breathing heavy and noisy, a noise which penetrated everywhere, even before he did.

"My story reached there before I did," the singer sang out and I stopped the record player instantly.

"Hurry up, we have to go to see Oto."

Due to excessive drinking Herr Strein wasn't able to drive any more. My husband brought the car out and Herr Strein, with his red nose, flopped on to the front seat. All through the way his loud snores battled to reach my nose, then my throat and then to push through my stomach. Before getting off at the vet's I had decided that I would never again travel with Herr Strein specially when he had been drinking.

Oto had died and his body placed in the car boot. All three of us sat in the car as we returned, I sat the back and my husband and Herr Strein at the front. Behind me was the rear window of the car and underneath it, the boot. In the boot lay Oto's body. I had never experienced travelling in such close proximity to a dead body. Herr Strein's breath kept exhaling its stinking smell of beer mingled with grief from the front seat. Oto's body and Herr Strein were taken to his house. My husband made coffee in Herr Strein's study and we all drank it in total silence, no, in an anguished quietness. While drinking it, I tried to hold my breath, afraid that creating the slightest noise might not be appropriate for such an atmosphere of mourning and might offend Herr Strein. There on the divan in the corner, over a wooden stool, was placed Oto's body. It was covered with a big, white, creamy, silky, satin frothlike cloth with frills. We sat there mute, drinking coffee, as if we were sitting in a cemetery.

Next day it was decided where the body was going to be buried. Herr Strein was so sad that, being his neighbours, we had to fulfil our duty and be with him throughout the entire business. A hole was dug under a chestnut tree and Oto's tiny body was laid to rest. The little coffin, made of walnut wood and wrapped in white frothy satin with frills, was carried by the two gentlemen. Herr Strein's nose was red from repeated blowing and his eyes were puffy. My husband had to hold his arms and help him to return to the car. When the shovel and other things had been put back in the car boot, we drove home. Again I sat at the back. It was the same journey back home. I kept receiving Herr Strein's beery breath in my nostrils all the way. My decision never to travel with him proved futile. I was forced, not only to take part in the burial with him, but also to accompany him to the Family Court the following day. On the elevated platform there was the chair of the judge and on either side of him sat his legal assistants. A little lower down sat the typist and the representative of the law. On the floor facing them were the audience and plaintiff. Exactly in the middle sat Elma with Comet, their son who was about four-and-a-half-years old. Due to her long illness, Elma seemed barely alive. She sat in the chair bent, like a tree which had been hit by a storm, and was about to fall at any moment. Her thin body had disappeared in the folds of her clothes. The same was true of Comet.

When we moved to Herr Strein's neighbourhood, he was already living alone. Elma and Comet had gone away from the house. I have personally heard him speak only once or twice about his wife and child. Now I was looking at them for the first time, face to face. Comet was the epitome of misery and helplessness. He was quiet, looked insecure and frightened, a child who would start at the slightest noise. His face was colourless and devoid of all emotions. He was sitting there, holding his sickly mother's hand, looking so terrified and devastated that everyone who looked at him felt sympathy towards him, but nobody could do anything. Who could interfere with the work of fate described by Omar Khayyam, "The moving finger writes and having writ moves on, nor all thy piety nor wit... can cancel half a line; nor all your tears wash out a word of it."

Two years ago, when Elma was admitted to hospital with breast cancer, it was hoped that after her operation she would recover fully. Little Comet was transferred from Herr Strein's house and placed in a Children's Home by the Social Services. After the operation, when Elma came back, she was very weak and looked terrible. Her hair had fallen out, her chest was flat and her face full of wrinkles. She looked like an old woman of seventy. Herr Strein was very sympathetic and visited her a few times. As he was extremely sensitive, he couldn't look at her and could not endure seeing her in such a horrible situation. So Elma was moved to a Social Service's flat. Little Comet went with her. For him that frail and aged-looking mother was the dearest person in the world. Her cancer had returned and according to the doctors, this time she would not survive. So the Family Court had summoned the parents and the social worker to decide little Comet's future.

It was a mere legal formality. Comet's future was decided. He would be sent to a Children's Home. Elma was sitting there, drooping like a broken tree, as if finding it difficult to remain seated. Comet was keeping his strong hold on her arms, his face even paler. He seemed like a ball, torn and faded, which had been continuously knocked about by other people. Agony and anguish were evident in his eyes. Large in their sockets, they looked terrified and restless, always moving. He would look at the floor, then at the ceiling, and the platform where the judge sat, at the people around him, who sat indifferent and aloof, in the callous quietness of the room. His eyes would look everywhere, then come back to his weak and weary mother. The anxiety in them might lessen but the grip on his mother's hand would tighten, turning his knuckles white.

The court gave its verdict and Herr Strein went outside. He was alone, and right now grief-stricken, because of Oto's death. How could he have taken the responsibility of a sickly and weak child like Comet on his own? The child's mother had been told that she was going to live only for so many months and days. The doctors were united in saying that. For that child, only a social worker could be a suitable solution. Therefore, the court made Comet a ward of the Social Services.

The woman was like a fallen tree and in the tight grip of death. Her desolate eyes were white with terror. Despair was like a sharp knife twisting and turning in those eyes. The eyes of the little boy

were stunned, terrified and restless. Like a drill, they looked at the Judge; towards the Court and Herr Strein; they drilled holes in every face and in every heart. It went deep inside the heart and tore everything apart. The two holes drilled into my heart by those pleading eyes will perhaps never close and the wound will never heal. It will, throughout my life, bleed slowly.

In one hole, there stands a child. Although he is quiet, his heart-rending cry, suppressed on his lips, is pleading that he doesn't want to go with the social worker. He stands there helpless and dry-eyed. Hiding behind his eyes there are ferocious waves of a raging sea of unshed tears. Those sorrowful eyes watch the people and the scene around him. In the other hole there is his little hand in his cancer-stricken mother's skeletal hand, holding it perhaps for the last time. There is the dying mother and her silence, muted and helpless. Then she loosens the grip and lets his hand go as if she is shedding blood from her eyes. Her look was like a cry of desperation, then slowly she walked towards the door as if going to her final destination. That silent cry was like a tornado which gripped everything in sight. With these two scenes lodged in my heart like two black holes, I proceeded to the parking lot where my husband was sitting in the car with Herr Strein.

On the tree trunk a small rectangular space was cleared and special words were written with golden paint. To search for that special paint we had to go to a Super Store. When morning became afternoon, we had lunch in the restaurant of that Super Store. Finally, Herr Strein gave his approval for the paint and we reached the cemetery in the late afternoon. Now the inscription had been completed and the writing had almost dried. We stood back a few paces and inspected our work.

"Oto was bought at his birth by Herr Strein, at an exorbitant price. He was small, of a mixed breed, a rare and experimental animal. For the last eighteen months he was looked after with extreme care and lived in comfort. There was always a vet to care for him. Alas, he did not live long — our dear Oto, is buried here!"

(The title of the story in Urdu is *Deedaye Ter.*)